SPIDER DEMON'S KISS

By
Alex McAnders

McAnders Books

*****

Official Website: www.AlexAndersBooks.com
Podcast: BisexualRealTalk
Visit Alex Anders at: Facebook.com/AlexAndersBooks & Instagram
Get 6 FREE ebooks and an audiobook by signing up for Alex Anders' mailing list at: AlexAndersBooks.com

Published by McAnders Publishing

Titles by Alex McAnders

M/M Wolf Shifter

Spider Demon's Kiss
His Wolf Protector & Audiobook
His Caged Wolf & Audiobook; Book 2 & Audiobook;
Book 3 & Audiobook; Book 4 & Audiobook; Book 5

SPIDER DEMON'S KISS

Chapter 1

Dante

*****Author note: When you are done reading this story, you can extend your reading experience by filling quiet nights chatting, flirting, or having sexy talk with the characters from this book on the author's new A.I. website, BookishBoyfriend.com.**

I swear, and God knows I love him, but if Matteo's hairy wolf ass turned up dead in a ditch, my life would be so much easier. Don't get me wrong, the streets of New York would run red with the blood I spill getting revenge. No one touches one of my pack, much less my brother. But even that would be easier than cleaning up his messes.

"You don't know what happened," Matteo claimed, his newly acquired nose ring becoming the only thing I can see.

"I don't care what happened. You're a goddamn Ricci. The man your wolf killed and then you dragged through the streets was a Yakuza made man."

"Dante…"

"I don't want to hear it!" I said hearing enough.

Standing with my fist on my desk was the only thing that prevented me from shifting and ripping out his throat. Knowing him, he'd probably be fine with it as long as I didn't touch his annoyingly perfect nose. The man protected his face in a fight like it was his goddamn money-maker.

"Look, our familial ties are the only thing stopping me from feeding you to those goddamn cursed spooks myself."

"You didn't hear what he did to the girl," Matteo claimed not backing down.

"I don't care if he dismembered her limb from limb."

"You don't mean that."

"I'm saying it, ain't I?"

"You say a lot of things. But you're a lighter touch than I am."

"I swear to God, Matteo!"

"It was Vincente's little sister!" Matteo yelled stopping me in my tracks.

"What?"

"Yeah. You remember her, right? It was the little girl whose wolf would run with our pack when she barely knew what shifting was. Seems that someone spread word around that she liked it rough. Then that figlio di puttana corners her high out of his mind and messed her up. She's got scars that her shifting won't heal."

I could feel my wolf fighting its way out just hearing about it. The truth is I remember that girl. Back when I knew her, she had pigtails and hero worship for anyone in a pack. Anyone who would take advantage of her like that had to die.

Matteo wasn't wrong for ridding the planet of scum like that. Hell, if I heard about it first, I would have done it myself. But there were ways of doing it that didn't lead to an all-out turf war.

Nobody likes it, but the Yakuza are a reality in New York and there's no getting rid of them. Any opium that hits the streets is their doing. Global trade is beyond the reach of any wolf pack not named Lyon or Clément.

But with the head of the Lyon family gone and no one willing to take over, that just leaves the Cléments. They would have been the most likely to take control if not for two things. Armand has no male heirs, and word is that he now has a rat problem.

That void is an opportunity. Someone will step up. Who better than the Ricci pack? Thanks to Papa releasing his grip on dealings, I've managed to extend our reach. Construction, lending, we've even made strides into diamonds. But one thing we can't do is heroin.

First off, it's nasty shit that leaves a city worse than you found it. That's something my father would have done. But now we're in the growth industry. We build things. We lend the money that makes the city better.

Those foreign spooks are using our city as their toilet. We can't let that happen. But Matteo's hot head just gave them the excuse they've been looking for to declare war. That's not good for Ricci business.

"Look, Matteo, there are ways of doing things," I said calming down.

"Yeah. The way I did it makes sure that no one will think twice about doing it again."

Heat rushed through me calling my wolf. In sudden blind rage my fist nearly shattered the desk.

"No! He was a fuckin' made man! Do you know what a fuckin' made man is?"

Matteo wilted seeing I had lost it.

"I know what a made man is, Dante."

"What is a fuckin' made man?"

"It means he's untouchable."

"No! It means that if you touch him, someone's head has to roll. Someone has to die. That's it. No negotiation. Your action killed one of our men. Some goddamn kid is going to grow up without a father because of you. Did you take one second to consider that?"

"You didn't see what he did to Vincente's sister," he said losing his asshole bravado.

"There are ways of doing it," I said feeling the anger threatening to bubble up again.

"Alright, alright. I made a mistake. I screwed up. You could work your magic and get us out of this, can't you?"

Seeing humility on Matteo was a new look. It caught me off guard pushing me back into my seat. Was this what would finally sink in for the man who couldn't learn a lesson that didn't involve hair gel?

"Come on, Dante. You can handle this, right? That fuck had it comin'. None of our men need to die for that."

I stared at him seeing something I never saw in my younger brother before. I had never heard him talk like this. Was that fucker softening? He could use a few rounded edges. My life would be a lot easier if they were.

"You're gonna be the death of me," I said relenting.

Matteo beamed that goddamn smile that was usually the last thing his victims saw before his wolf lunged for their throat.

"I knew you could handle things. That's why you got the tough job. Pa had it right when he put you in charge. You're exactly who this family needs."

"You're a shit kiss-ass," I told him, my mind swirling in search of a solution.

"I'm gonna leave you to it. If there's anything you need me to do, you know I'm there for you."

"You could hand yourself over to them and save me the trouble of knocking you out and taking you."

Matteo froze not sure if I was joking.

"Don't kid like that, Dante. One of our men might overhear and think you're serious."

"Oh, I am serious," I said imagining my easier life. "I'd even put a little bow on you so they could open you under a tree."

"Do those Japanese fucks even celebrate Christmas?"

"You better hope not. I could get my shopping finished real early."

Matteo stared at me side-eyed.

"Don't joke like that," he said flashing signs of the wolf I had no choice but to love.

Any hint of restitution was gone. Instead of learning from this, had he simply become a better actor? Maybe I should give him to the Yakuza. Would anyone blame me? That man had a sadistic streak that no one would miss.

"I'll take care of it," I told him, not knowing how, but sure I would.

"Thanks. But, I need to tell you, don't ever question my judgment like that. It doesn't feel good."

I stared at him giving him nothing in response. That was usually the best way to deal with his crazy. It was like there were two people living in his body. One that would rip out a man's throat for looking at him funny. The other, the scared little boy I protected from Pa. There was no telling when either would come out, especially when he shifted.

Pa had done a number on all of his kids. None of us were affected more by it than Matteo was. There was definitely something wrong with our old man. Whatever it was, he passed on to Matteo. In ways, Matteo was becoming more like him every day. All I was left with was hope.

I was sure I could reach him before Pa's grip was complete. There was still a good man in there somewhere. Until I found it, he was gonna tie corpses to the back of his car and drag them through Yakuza territory.

The thought of what he had done flowed over me. "Shit! How the fuck am I gonna get us out of this?"

The answer came to me as fast as I asked it.

Two years ago, when I took over the reins for the family, I had a visit from Sato. The Yakuza hadn't yet gotten their foothold on New York's heroin trade and the old man was grasping at straws. The word was his bosses were considering recalling him in the permanent sort of way. So Sato was fighting for his life.

The man had vision, I'll give him that much. He saw the downfall of the Lyon's coming a mile away and he proposed an alliance. But he didn't just want our word. Those cursed spooks never did anything half way. He wanted family ties. He offered me his daughter in marriage.

My response was, "Fuck, no!"

I'll admit, it was not my finest moment. To be fair, I was going through some things at the time. I was under a lot of pressure to take over and I saw marriage as the off switch to my pressure release valve.

Sure, I saw myself marrying someday. But, for my wolf not to murder anyone who looked at me funny, I needed certain outlets. That required the right kind of marriage. She didn't have to be a wolf, but she did have to be able to turn a blind eye.

It turned out that Yuki was exactly who I needed. I hadn't met her at that time. I think he said she was still in Japan. But seeing her at a ribbon cutting ceremony as their family's representative, I knew I had made a mistake in refusing her.

At the ceremony, I didn't see her look into a man's eye once. It was all bows and humility. Japanese culture is very different from ours. I see that now. Turns out, she would have been the perfect wife. And now, it looks like she will be.

It didn't even matter that Sato's entire lineage was cursed. If they hadn't already, all of his offspring would become possessed.

That wasn't necessary a bad thing. There were spirits and there were demons. I'm told that Sato was a crow demon. That explained his ruthlessness and blind ambition. But a woman like Yuki could end up with a house spirit or something. One of those would bring the owner of the household success and good luck.

I didn't know any of this when Sato offered me Yuki. And as insulted as he was by my rejection, Sato hadn't shut the door on his idea. The man's life was at stake. He couldn't afford to start a war over honor. So, two years later, here we are.

Number one, Matteo has made us indebted to the Yakuza. Number two, their global trade would cement the Ricci's hold on the city. And number three, I still didn't have a wife. It was just the wrong time before. Sato would understand that, right?

Cursed or not, Sato was still Japanese. Wasn't being patient a Japanese thing? That's why they made those designs in the sand, right? Shit, I didn't know. If I was gonna marry Yuki, I was gonna need to know this stuff.

"You cannot marry that curse into our pack," Pa declared from the head of the table at Sunday dinner.

'How the fuck did he know about that?' I wondered looking around at the assembled Ricci boys who filled their plates as if my getting married was old news. There was only one of my brothers I trusted with this, Lorenzo. And like usual, he wasn't here.

"You marrying a Sato?" Matteo asked with a smirk. "When the fuck did this happen?"

"Ever since my shit for brains brother killed a made man and I had to clean up his mess," I spit melting his smirk.

"Oh."

"Yeah. That's what I thought," I said looking at my remaining three brothers as they quickly averted their eyes.

"That cursed demon can't be trusted," Pa proclaimed like the oracle on the mound.

"Yeah, Pa? Then what do you suppose I do?"

"Go to war. Or will you shame me as a son who is afraid to fight?"

"He's not afraid to fight, Pa," Matteo said again showing me glimpses of a new man. "Dante would fight the best of them. He's just fighting them in a different way."

Was Matteo finally getting it?

"Only a coward runs from war," Pa declared.

"And only a fool runs into one," I told him not backing down.

"They will humiliate you. They will humiliate our pack, and we'll end up exactly where we started."

My wolf's fury blinded me. Slamming my fist in front of me, I shattered my plate sending food everywhere.

"Dante!" Ma yelled thinking she could control things like when I was five.

"No, Ma! I've had it with this shit," I said getting up.

"Dante, sit down!" Ma insisted.

"I don't mean to disrespect you, Ma, but this is ending right now."

"And what is it that you're ending?" Pa asked with more calm than he had a right to have.

That told me what he was thinking. Pa was built for confrontation. His wolf lived for it. He made our wolves into the killers they were with the broad side of a bat and the lit end of cigarette butts. While he did, he never flinched, just like he didn't now.

Staring at him, he reminded me of the stakes. If you come at the king, you best not miss. Pa had us late in life but he wasn't an old wolf. At least, not old enough to expect him to go off quietly. When he looked in the mirror, he didn't see the grey hair and relentless wrinkles. He saw himself as a man who could take me.

Calming myself, I took a breath and then brushed speckles of Ma's marinara from my vest.

"This second-guessing ends now," I told Pa not needing to look at him. "Your role as the head of this pack is complete. You will always be our father and we give you the respect you deserve for it. But when it comes to running pack business, that job is mine now."

"I haven't given you it, son," he said coldly.

I looked at him assured.

"You don't have to give it to me, Pa. I'm taking it," I said whipping off my vest and shirt and shifting before Pa knew what was happening.

I knew what I looked like to human eyes. I was big. I always had been. My wolf took up space, so when I jumped onto the dinner table and locked my eyes on Pa's challenging him, everyone backed away.

Staring at my father who remained in human form, I crouched approaching him. I wasn't gonna underestimate him. As fast as I could shift, Pa was faster. I had learned the trick from him. If I looked away for a moment, I could turn back finding his fangs lunging towards me. So instead, I stared, approached, and growled.

Just out of reach of Pa's knife, I stopped. I was close enough. He, like everyone, knew what I was doing. If he thought he still had it in him, this was his time. If he didn't at least shift, his hold on the pack was over. To fight and lose was one thing. To not even step into the ring was another.

When long enough had passed that Pa would no longer be able to recover his reputation, I next turned to my brothers. If there was someone else who thought they had what it took, this was their time. No one challenged.

I next turned to Matteo. If anyone thought they could take me, it was him. Standing on the opposite side of his overturned chair, he only stared back.

This was it. This was the moment. I was now the unchallenged head of our pack. From this point on, things were gonna be different. There would be no one second guessing my decisions. If they did, it wouldn't be just me, they would have the whole pack to deal with.

Jumping off the table and shifting, I stared back at my family as I pulled on my pants and got dressed. It was never as intimidating watching someone get dressed as the shift itself so I filled the space with my plan.

"Now, I will be cleaning up our pack's mess by getting married. You can get on board with it or not. Frankly, I don't give a shit. This pack needs to be led into the future. And the old ways of doing things are done.

"If any of you would like to come to the wedding, I'll send you an invitation. If not, who the fuck cares? Either way, you will respect me. And as the new head of the pack, you will do what I say."

With that, I adjusted my jacket, gave a final look at my stunned family and left.

I took a deep breath making sure to fill my lungs with the sweet smell of the Brooklyn streets as I descended the stairs to the sidewalk. Why? Because I knew the scent could be my last. No one talked to my father the way I just had. At least, no one who lived to talk about it.

My being his son didn't make a difference. Word was that Pa once tried to kill his own brother. No one could confirm it because his brother disappeared soon after. The thought was that he moved back to Italy.

Every so often we would hear from him. Mostly during the holiday season. It usually came with a request for safe passage back into the country. But the fact that I've never met him, speaks to my father's ability to hold a grudge.

Rounding the sidewalk, I started to believe that I had done it. I had claimed the pack and he had accepted it. In his lack of immediate action, he had declared me the victor. I officially had the reins of the Ricci pack. And my first official act would be marrying the woman who would allow my true life to begin.

"Dante!" I heard yelled as I was about to get into my car.

I braced myself. Would I turn around to the wild eyes of a charging wolf? Whose would it be? Would it be Matteo's? I should have considered the grip Pa had on him.

With not enough time to shift, I steeled my spine and spun finding a surprise.

"Lorenzo! What's going on?" I asked, seeing the brother who avoided these dinners as if it were wolfsbane.

"We need to talk," he said approaching.

"Alright. Not here," I replied scanning the streets and ushering him into my car.

Quickly pulling away, the brownstones whipped by us.

"What is it?" I said keeping one eye on the rearview mirror.

"There's word on the street. It's about your upcoming marriage."

"How is my marriage word on the street? I only finalized that deal six hours ago," I said not liking where this was going.

"If you think you finalized it, you might need to talk to Sato again."

"And why is that?" I said feeling my neck warm.

"Don't kill the messenger, Dante," Lorenzo warned nervously, his lack of tattoos and lean build striking a strong contrast to Matteo and me.

"Why would I kill the messenger?"

"Because Sato doesn't plan on offering you Yuki. He's offering you Kuroi."

My brother could not have missed how white I turned. My face tingled as I slowly left my body.

"Dante, did you hear me?"

"I heard you."

"He's trying to humiliate our pack," Lorenzo said pointing out the obvious.

It looks like Sato hadn't gotten over me refusing his first marriage offer. This was how he was getting revenge. His demon wanted war for what Matteo had done to his man. And the only way out of it was for me to marry his son, the spider demon.

"You're not thinking about doing it, are you, Dante?"

I looked away as Pa's words echoed in my head. He had been right about Sato. Fuck!

So, what did I do now? If I didn't go through with it, my father would use it to undermine my still tenuous control over the pack.

If I did marry Sato's bastard off-spring, the chances of me ending up dead like all of his other lovers were damn near certain.

Maybe I was thinking about this wrong. Maybe all of the bat-shit crazy things I heard about Kuroi weren't true. Maybe everything going around about him was an exaggeration.

The street has been known to get things mixed up on occasion. What I heard about Kuroi could be one of those times. Because no one could be as out of their mind as he was supposed to be, could they?

Chapter 2

Kuroi

'If I had a dollar for every time balls were stuffed in my mouth at the most inopportune time,' I considered with a laugh.

Although, the one currently prying my mouth open was my fault

, I had sworn off being hog-tied naked in the trunk of a car a long time ago. It's the only way to keep birthday memories special.

So, why was I now blindfolded, and ball gagged in what had to be a two-year-old E-class? Who the fuck knows? Thirty minutes ago I was very happily attached to a Saint Andrew's Cross. I mean, I'm all about pushing limits. But if tonight ends with my dead body being dumped in a ditch, I will be so pissed.

Once the brakes tightened on my chariot and we rolled to a stop, it was only a second before sunlight touched my naked flesh. I could feel two people looking down at me. They were wondering what to do.

Because they were quiet, I had to assume they were using gestures. Interesting! That meant that they weren't planning on killing me and they hoped to survive our little encounter. How cute!

When one of them grabbed me by the legs and threw me over his shoulder, I knew exactly where I was going. The switch from sunlight to cool air confirmed it. If I hadn't been blinded with hope that my lover had finally gotten creative, I would have noticed it before.

There was only one person whose tasteless cologne stuck to anyone who was in the same room as them. And the wave of scent that tickled my nose as I was lowered onto a chair confirmed it. With my ball gag removed, I swallowed and wet my lips.

"Hello, father," I said not needing to smell or hear him to know he was there.

"Why is he naked?" Father asked addressing his men.

"The question is, why aren't you? This is a party, isn't it? At least, that was where I was before your men decided it was a good day to die."

"We found him that way, Boss," one of them said with the appropriate amount of fear in his voice.

"I was in the middle of something," I informed dear old dad.

"And why isn't he dressed?"

"We thought it was better to keep him restrained to keep him from, you know…"

"Killing you? Oh, it's too late for that," I said with a smile.

"Untie him. Get him dressed," Father said headed for the door foolishly leaving the three of us alone.

"You heard my father." I imitated my father's ascent and righteous tone. "Untie me! Get me dressed!"

Neither of them moved. Still blindfolded, I assumed they were gesturing again.

"I know. Tough choice. Do you untie my hands first? No, I could do too much with my hands. Then, what about my feet? But, I could run. The boss wouldn't like that. What to do? What to do?" I taunted.

After what felt like way too much staring, my scared friend opted to start with my feet. Tugging and pulling on the well-secured knot, it must have been as much of a surprise to him as it was to me that the ropes fell to the ground and my lean legs rose and clamped around his neck.

Did I say surprise? I meant inevitable. How else was I going to kill him? My hands were still tied. My legs were all I had.

Feeling the slight shift of his body weight, I twisted catching him off guard and spinning him onto his back. I did another obvious thing after that, I let him go, slipped my tied hands under my ass and used the rope binding them to choke him lifeless.

I didn't quite get to lifeless because I wasn't a miracle worker. I still had a second man to deal with. Not knowing where he was, I could have removed the blindfold. But where was the fun in that? Didn't they call me the spider demon behind my back? How could they continue to if Mama didn't feed?

Hearing a quick inhale, I sprung across the room and went to work. First, I took out his legs hearing a bone snap. Grunts and moans followed. It served him right for being so fragile. That's the problem with toys. They break so easily.

'I know, father, this is why we can't have nice things.'

My father never actually told me that. I like to pretend. In another life, I had a father who changed into his smoking jacket when he got home and lit his pipe. The economy blah, blah, blah. Pork bellies.

'I hit a homerun in the game today, Father.'

'You did? Well, let me give you a firm handshake. The boys at school must be so envious of you.'

'Oh, they are father. Proper jealous,' I imagined as I hear another bone snap.

"Kuroi!" another familiar voice said ripping me from my flow. "Kuroi!"

Removing my thumb from the man's eye socket, I turned toward the voice and stood up.

"Why must you do this?"

"Why must I have a little fun?" I asked lifting my blindfold to see Yuki standing in front of me. "Man can't live on bread alone, sister."

Getting an eye-full of her naked little brother, Yuki averted her eyes.

"Something here you haven't seen before?" I said with a chuckle.

"Please, Kuroi, get dressed," she said holding a change of clothes in front of her.

"You're such a prude," I said to the woman who had never seen a dick in her life.

"You can't keep dishonoring father like this," she said as if sharing a fact.

"Why not? Father has no problem dishonoring me."

"You deserve better, Kuroi."

"We get what we deserve."

"You didn't deserve any of this."

"Yuki, didn't you know? This is what happens when your mother is a whore."

"Don't say that."

"Well, she was, wasn't she? Our father's whore. And this is what little bastards like me get."

Silence drew out between us as I got dressed.

Fine, I'll admit it. I'm not in the best mood. There was a reason father's men found me where I was. I can't always be the ball of sunshine I am without a little release. Father had interrupted my release. Now I was tense.

Sliding into the silk suit Yuki had handed me, I patted at my unruly hair and exited father's museum-sized office. Crossing the hallway with my obedient sister in tow, we approached my room and I headed to the mirror.

My reflection made me sick to look at. All of my siblings were fine porcelain dolls. Even my brothers. I was burnt ceramic. Instead of lying submissive and perfect, like a proper Japanese, my hair was a wired scrub brush sitting on my head.

Barely hiding my disgust, my focus shifted catching Yuki staring back at me in the mirror.

"Well, don't you look creepy," I said not getting Yuki to look away.

"I have something to tell you."

Turning back to the mirror, I pushed my fingers into my curls picking them out.

"And what's that?"

"Father plans on marrying you off."

As if she had choked the life out of me, the blood drained from my face.

"I begged him not to."

My mind swirled. What was going on? Married? Me?

"If he expects me to give him an heir…" I began struggling to remain on my feet.

"It's not that type of marriage," Yuki said lowering her head.

"I see. And what type of marriage is it."

"It's to the head of the Ricci family."

Picturing who that was, I almost laughed. It was to one of those crazy wolf shifters my father did business with. He didn't have his father's brutal reputation but he wasn't much better.

"So, I am again to be our father's whore. Like mother, like son."

"It won't be so bad. And I'm sure it won't last long."

"You mean because I'll kill him?" I asked feeling the spider demon rest its legs on my shoulders as I stared at her.

Yuki didn't respond. What could she say? Instead, I spoke.

"And when is this meant to happen?"

"Tonight."

"Tonight?" I coughed in shock. "He really wants this man dead, doesn't he?"

Yuki's eyes met the ground. I laughed. My father was marrying me off to a straight wolf shifter. Why would my husband-to-be agree to this? Does he even know I'm a man?

What happens when he finds out? And am I supposed to go without sex until one of us dies? If I get my needs met elsewhere, will he eat me?

His name was Dante, wasn't it? He was certainly the hot one in that family. Chiseled body, icy eyes, and ink from neck to wrist. I wouldn't mind him treating me like his bitch in one way. I wonder how long it would take him to remember I have a dick.

Pulling off my jacket, I headed to the closet.

"What are you doing?"

Turning around recapturing my humor, I replied, "It's my wedding day, Sister. I'm getting dressed."

I was going to make this a day to remember.

Chapter 3

Dante

This isn't good. None of this is fuckin' good. Sato has made me wait two days for a face-to-face with him to get this marriage shit straightened out and I don't like it.

As stressful as things are after Matteo did what he did, I wasn't lookin' to die. Maybe the rumors about Kuroi were true. Maybe they weren't. But if being married to Kuroi didn't get me killed, marrying a man would. There would be a target on my back, most of all from Pa.

He wouldn't be able to stand for this insult to the pack. And how would the men I demand respect from react to me being with a man? Weakness is something that will get you killed in my line of work. So there is no way this can happen.

The problem, though, is that that Yakuza son-of-a-bitch won't even talk to me about it. Yeah, he pretends that he doesn't speak English, but I know he understands every goddamn word I say. Play ignorant. That's how they underestimate you. Well, guess what, fucker, I know that game too and I'm not falling for it.

"You okay, Dante?" Lorenzo asked from the passenger seat. "You're looking a little red."

"I'm fine," I tell him definitely not feeling fine.

I felt like my face was on fire and bugs were crawling under my skin. This was exactly how I felt when my wolf was forcing me to shift. I guess my wolf had its own ideas about how to handle things. But if I let him take control, everyone would end up dead.

"You sure your contacts don't have anything we could use in this meeting?" I asked hoping a miracle would get me out of this.

"They got nothin'. I approached this from every angle I could think of. Sato isn't in debt to any New York packs. There are no dock workers that they rely on for their imports that we could squeeze, and with the structure of their compound, extermination wasn't an option."

I looked over at Lorenzo. I was impressed. He really had considered all of the angles. If something happened to me, he should be the one to lead the pack.

He could never do it. Leading a pack required as much intimidation as it did navigating obstacles. Lorenzo was a master at working behind the scenes. Maybe even better than me. But that was where his skills ended.

To lead a pack, you had to be a people person. Lorenzo wasn't that. Being a people person was Matteo in a nutshell. But Matteo was a hammer that looked at everything and everyone as a nail. If I could figure out how to combine those two brothers, they might be better than I could ever be. But you can't expect blood from a stone. With those two, you just have to take what you can get.

"That's disappointing, Lorenzo. I was counting on you coming through for me."

"I can only give you what I've found. Making up shit would just get you killed."

"In this situation, that isn't the only thing."

Pulling up to Sato's residence I had to marvel at it. He had somehow recreated Japan in upstate New York. It didn't entirely work. To be honest, Sato's compound looked like one of those 1920s American castles with the roofs replaced to make them do that Japanese swooping thing.

The garden was incredible, though. There were ponds and those manicured trees that looked like the tail of a poodle. In the front was sand with lines drawn in it and a large rock sticking out. And there was even one of those structures that look like Japanese writing. I didn't see what the purpose of it was other than to look nice. But everything told a story.

The story this told was that Sato was a man who did everything he could to pretend he wasn't where he was. My guess was that there was rage behind his expressionless exterior. There had to be a way I could use that to get out of this marriage. But how?

"Dante Ricci and family here to see Sato," I said to the com box outside the gate.

"Park. Security will meet you there," someone replied in a Japanese accent.

I turned to Lorenzo.

"Here goes nothing."

"You sure it won't be better to take care of this silently?"

"If you're asking if it would be better to put a hit on a man with some of the best security in the city, I'm sure," I said seeing a flash of our Pa in him.

"Think about it," he said leaning forward to get a better look at the place. "We could put a sniper in one of those tree-lines. Or, it doesn't have to be here. There are unguarded roofs around his office. With the right shooter, we could solve this problem in a second."

I looked at Lorenzo feeling my heart thump. There was no mistaking that he was our father's son.

"Don't even think about it, Lorenzo. Or better yet, think about what comes after that. You think his people back in Japan wouldn't be able to piece together his elimination with a forced marriage proposal? How long will it take for shit to hit the fan?

"There are better ways to handle things, Lorenzo. I tell ya, you and Matteo are exactly alike."

"Don't you compare me to that piece of shit."

"Hey, watch the way you talk about your brother."

"What are you talking about? You call him that all of the time."

"That's because I'm the one who has to keep cleaning up his messes. When that's your job, then you can say it. Until then, he's your brother and you love him."

"Whatever," Lorenzo replied sinking back into his chair.

It probably wasn't the best idea to piss off the only backup I would have if things went belly up. But Matteo needed as many people on his side as possible. I couldn't let Lorenzo write him off like that.

Exiting the car, four of Sato's men met us. I was sure that someone inside thought this would be an impressive show of force. Truth was, if I shifted, these four wouldn't even slow me down.

"Guns?"

"We're not giving you our fuckin' guns," Lorenzo snapped.

"Lorenzo, give them your fuckin' gun," I ordered reaching for mine. "We are entering Sato's home. We need to show him the respect he deserves."

Oh yeah, Lorenzo was pissed at me. Big fuckin' deal. He'll get over it.

The inside of Sato's house was as impressive as the garden. There wasn't much he could do with the 1920s architecture, but he made it work. The hard wood beams that traversed the ceiling, the minimalist design tiles and wooden décor, it felt like I was in a different world.

"This way please," the largest of the men said ushering me onto a balcony overlooking acres of land.

There was a man already there. Not Sato. Someone else. He stood humbly wearing what looked like a Japanese ceremonial gown and he had a book in his hand.

"You, there," Sato's security guy said gesturing for me to stand next to the man. "You, there," he said ushering Lorenzo to the side.

Lorenzo looked at me asking if he should go. I nodded and approached who I assumed was Sato's interrupter. Because, of course, Sato didn't speak English. Yeah, whatever.

It took about a minute of standing awkwardly with this man for Sato to arrive. Strangely, he didn't look at me. With his eyes averted, he took a position more than an arm's length away on the other side of the balcony as Lorenzo.

What was going on? I knew that Japanese culture had a lot of customs like bowing and shit, and a lot of it stretched into business. But I didn't know enough to say how weird this was.

It got even weirder when music began playing. Any music at a negotiation would be strange. But they were playing that wah-wah music. You know, it's that music they play in the quiet moments in Samurai movies. Why were they playing it now?

When someone else entered the balcony, I had a pretty good guess about what was going on. I don't know who it fuckin' was, but that fucker was wearing a Japanese wedding dress. I recognized that shit. And they were carrying a bouquet.

"Oh, no. Sato, no." I protested never taking my eyes off of my bride.

Sato grunted. It was loud. I think that fucker just chastised me in Japanese. Who the fuck did he think he was?

I was about to show him what I thought about this stunt by shoving my fist down his throat when my bride's stomping shoes grabbed my attention. It was the sound of wood on wood.

Staring at my bride again, my wolf stirred. Who was this? You would think I could tell by looking at them. But the dress, or gown, or whatever it was practically took up half of the room. Added to that was that there wasn't much of my bride showing. They didn't wear a veil, but the funny looking hat they wore covered their hair, while their makeup painted their face white.

Was this Yuki? Had Sato come to his senses and given me my perfect bride?

As my bride slowly approached, I looked closer. I couldn't be sure, but it did look like her. Goddamn were they beautiful, though. The robe they wore on top of their layered dress was embroidered with gold and blue images of ancient Japan. There were a lot of birds on it too. Or, maybe they were cranes?

Whatever they were, it was my bride's eyes that really got me. They stared at me not backing down. They were fierce and wild and staring into them did something to me. They made my wolf want to tear this place apart. But not to get away from them. My wolf would destroy the world to make them his.

When my bride stood in front of me and the man, I finally realized who the man was. He wasn't Sato's interrupter. He was a priest.

This was it. There was never going to be a negotiation. Sato had gotten me here for the ceremony. And when the priest began speaking in Japanese, I realized that if I didn't do something to stop this, in a minute, I was going to be married.

But to who? Yuki? It couldn't be. Not with eyes like that. Oh my god, those fuckin' eyes. I got hard just lookin' at them. What the fuck was goin' on?

With my bride's eyes still intensely focused on me, they nodded. What was that? What had just happened?

"Hai," my bride said.

Oh shit. Was that, I do?

The priest's face tilted towards me. He was saying something and I didn't know what the fuck it was. He could have been asking me for my left nut for all I knew. And when he stopped talking was when things got insane as fuck.

"I think you're getting married, bro," the brilliant Lorenzo informed me.

"No shit!" I said in a panic.

"What do you want to do?" he said his wolf perched ready to come out. "We could get the fuck out of here. Just say the word."

"Just give me a second," I said, my heart thumping.

I should get the fuck out of here, right? This was bullshit. I didn't agree to this.

On the other hand, there were those fuckin' eyes. They were doin' something to me. My wolf wanted to rip the fuckin' dress off her and tear her apart. But was it a her? Was it a him?

Kuroi was a him. I had seen him before. Brown skin. Delicate hands. And… oh shit, those fuckin' eyes. I was staring into Kuroi's eyes.

Before I knew it, I said it. I don't even remember doing it. I just know I did.

Was it Hai or Hi? I may as well have said, "I do."

Did I? I did. I just married Kuroi Sato, the fucking spider demon. What the fuck was I doing?

Before I could figure it out, Yuki entered. There was no confusing the two. With her head bowed, she shuffled in with a tray of shots. Two shots. It was a weird time for it. But after what I had just done, I would take anything with kick.

When Yuki approached, the priest gestured for me to take one. I did. So did the person standing in front of me. The priest gestured for me to drink. Kuroi stared me in the eyes waiting. Was this it? Was this the final, I do? If I didn't do this, could I still walk away?

With the shot glass in my hand, I raised it. Looking into those mesmerizing eyes, I lifted the glass to my lips. In mirroring succession, Kuroi tilted his head back. The sweet alcohol slipped down my throat.

"Hai," Sato said who having witnessed enough, turned to go.

That was it. I had done it. I was married. What had I done?

Staring at my bride, my mind swirled. What was I supposed to do now? I could figure my way out of this. I was sure of it. And as my brain began churning out a myriad of plans, my bride leaned forward and kissed me.

Soft, gentle. Those were his lips. His lips, not hers. In a second, I found his neck in my hand. It was small, narrow. My thumb pressed against his jaw. I could feel it open. Losing myself, I felt my tongue enter.

Alive. I felt so alive. As our two tongues met, they danced. It was so hot my head hurt. It was the type of kiss that there was no coming back from. It made my wolf howl.

He was small. I could have crushed him in my hands. I could have consumed him. I wanted every inch of him, possessed, and marked as mine. My heart's thumping told me that. And when I released him, when I let go of his touch, I was awake.

"Dante?" Lorenzo said crashing me back to reality.

Oh fuck! What had I done?

A wave of heat rushed over me. It was overwhelming. I shouldn't be here. I shouldn't be doing this. Not now. Not in front of anybody.

They couldn't see me like this. No one can. More than that, I could feel myself shifting. I don't know why, but I was. I had to get out of here. And turning to meet the shocked eyes of my brother, that's what I did.

Rushing off of the balcony and through the house, I ran for my car desperately trying to keep my wolf inside.

"Dante?" Lorenzo called after me.

I couldn't face him. Not now. I just needed to get away.

Grabbing my keys, I jumped into my car. Pressing the button and flooring the gas, I pulled away. If they hadn't opened the gate, I would have run it down. I didn't have to. And as the tree-lined street whipped past me, I rolled down the window to get air.

I couldn't breathe. Neither could my wolf. Why couldn't we breathe?

Fidgeting in my seat, I was doing everything trying to stop myself from shifting. At the same time, I was trying to put things together. I was Dante Ricci. I was the head of the Ricci pack. I didn't kiss men. I didn't…

That was when I felt it. A pinch to the neck. Had I been shot?

Touching the spot, I pulled my hand back. Was there blood on it or wasn't there? I couldn't tell. It was getting hard to see. Looking back up through the windshield I realized how fast I was going.

"Oh shit!" I exclaimed before I blacked out and heard a crash.

Chapter 4

Dante

'What happened?' I thought as my mind cleared from the haze of nothing. Where was I? The last thing I remembered was a wedding. No, wait, I was in a car. I was driving away from a wedding. No, I was driving away from my wedding.

Shit! That's right. I had gone to Sato's place to negotiate my way out of marrying his son and had ended up marrying him on the spot. Then, he kissed me, I ran, I felt what felt like a pinch to the neck and then things went dark.

I think I crashed my car. Was I still in my car?

Forcing my eyes to open, I didn't find my BMW. I was lying down in a white room. As things cleared, I saw a pulse monitor and a ceiling-level TV. I was in a hospital room and I felt like shit.

Looking around, I found only one person. It was Lorenzo. He was entertaining himself on his phone when the sound of my movement made him look up.

"Dante, you're awake. Thank God!" he said hurrying to my side.

I opened my mouth to ask him what the fuck was going on but nothing came out.

"Relax. I'll get the doctor. I was worried about you for a second there," he said with a smile before rushing out of the room.

He was worried about me? Why was that? Did other things happen after whoever it was shot me?

I needed to recover and I needed to do it fast. My best option was to shift. But reaching for my wolf, I could barely feel it. It was as weak as I was. It couldn't come out even if I wanted it to.

I felt drugged. They must have given me painkillers. That meant it would be hours before I could shift again. After that, I could get out of here, shift, and then figure out who shot me.

I was reaching across my body to feel where the bullet hit me when the door reopened and a doctor entered. She was a lot younger than I was used to my doctors looking. She was also distinctly not a wolf.

As far as I could smell, she was human. Of course, so was Sato. But that didn't stop him from being possessed by a demon.

"No, don't do that," she insisted, reaching out to stop my hand.

Not knowing the situation, I lowered my hand and again tried to speak.

"What happened?" I squeaked out, my throat feeling like a desert.

"You might need something to drink."

The small Indian lady turned to my brother.

"Do you mind telling one of the nurses at the stand to bring Mr. Ricci something to drink?"

"Of course."

"And, can you give us a minute once you do?" she requested causing Lorenzo's eyes to bounce to mine.

I gave him a nod and Lorenzo agreed. I figured, whatever the doctor knew was better kept between us, at least until I had time to eliminate a few potential shooters.

With my brother gone, the doctor approached the side of my bed. She had kind eyes and there was something about her I trusted.

"I'm Dr. Rohit. You're in Garrison Hospital Center because you were in a car accident," she explained.

"I hit something," I replied as my memories surfaced. "Was it a tree?"

"It was."

"Someone shot me and I passed out."

She looked at me confused. "I'm sorry?"

"Someone shot me. They hit me in the neck. It caused me to lose control."

Still confused, the doctor gently held my chin and turned my head. When she didn't find anything on one side, she tilted my chin to look at the other.

"Why do you think you were shot in the neck?" she asked with a furrowed brow.

"Cuz I felt it. It was right here," I said reaching for the spot again.

To my surprise, not only did my neck not hurt to touch, but there was nothing there. No wound, no bandage, nothing. And as far as I could tell from how the rest of my body felt, I hadn't shifted and healed it.

"I don't understand. I felt it."

"As far as our examiners have been able to tell, you haven't sustained any injury that might have broken the surface. You will probably have a bruise across your chest from the seat belt and your head might be a little foggy from the impact with the air bag. But, miraculously, other than that, you're fine."

"I'm fine?" I asked confused. "Then, why did I pass out?"

The doctor stuck her hands in her pockets and relaxed.

"Yes. That is why I requested that I speak to you alone."

"Okay," I asked bracing myself.

"I know how important image can be in your world…"

"What world is that?" I asked interrupting.

"I'm sure I don't know," she said backing off her position. "But, I thought you would want us to be alone when I told you that you crashed your car after blacking out from a panic attack."

Of all the things that she could have said, panic attack was nowhere on the list. I processed it for a second.

"No. What else you got?"

"I'm afraid this isn't a multiple choice situation."

"Nah. Can't be. I don't have panic attacks."

"Have you been under an increased amount of stress recently?"

Have I been under an increased amount of stress? Let me see. My idiot brother killed a Yakuza made man, I'm waiting for my father to make his move to remove me as alpha, and I was tricked into marrying a man who has killed all of his past lovers.

"Not more than usual," I told the doctor knowing it wasn't true.

"Nonetheless, all of your symptoms point to an acute panic attack that led to you feeling light-headed and briefly passing out, which led to you running into a tree. Did anything stressful happen right before the accident?"

Let's see, the man I married did kiss me in front of my brother and one of my biggest rivals, and it felt so good that my head almost exploded.

"Not that I can think of," I told the doctor.

"I see," the Doc said considering it. "Well, we're still running tests. But until we find contradicting results, I would recommend lowering your stress levels. Can you take some time off from your job? Is that possible right now?"

"That is absolutely not possible. And neither is the chance of me having a panic attack. I hope you didn't write that down in your records anywhere," I said as threateningly as I had intended it.

"You were brought in by a representative of the Sato family. And I can assure you that we will extend you the same privacy and discretion we show them."

Ah! Now I was getting it. This was Sato's doctor who, I was sure, would say anything Sato asked her to.

"I see," I said, my mind finally starting to click into gear. "But let's say that I hadn't had a panic attack. What else could it be?"

"What do you mean?"

I thought of Kuroi.

"There's a history of men in my situation having heart attacks. Could I have had something like that?"

The doctor gave me that confused look again. Why was she doing it?

"Yes, that is a possibility. But usually a man of your age and physical condition wouldn't be a candidate for a myocardial infarction. And we did run a test for markers of such an event and they were all negative."

"But, it could have been a heart attack?" I clarified.

"The symptoms did present in similar ways. But, like I said, the most likely cause remains a panic attack."

"So, either I had a panic attack, which, if true, would make me too weak to do a job as stressful as mine. Or, I had a heart attack under very suspicious circumstances. Is that right, Doc?"

"Panic attacks are very controllable with the right lifestyle changes and regulation techniques," she replied avoiding my question.

"I see. Tell me, Doc, is it also possible that I was shot with something. Not like a bullet, but maybe a dart or anything? Because I definitely felt something hit my neck. Is a pinch to the neck also something that comes with a panic attack?" I challenged.

"Not usually. But..."

"So, it's possible that something could have shot me in the neck as well."

"Mr. Ricci, I've found that the most likely cause is usually the right one."

"Just answer my question. Is a pinch on the neck also a symptom, or whatever you call it, of having a panic attack?"

"No, Mr. Ricci," she said relaxing in resignation.

"Could anything associated with a pinch to the neck lead to a heart attack that doesn't have what you were looking for? You know, what did you call them? Markers?"

Dr. Rohit paused.

"As I said, the most likely cause is usually the correct one…"

"Doc…" I protested not wanting to argue with her.

"…However, yes. A pinch to the neck could both be the cause of heart attack as well as a symptom of one depending on the cause."

"And what could cause something like that?"

The Doc shook her head reluctant to answer.

"A poison. But, Mr. Ricci, and I can't emphasize this enough. There has been no evidence of that and the most likely cause…"

"Is a panic attack. I know. When will I be able to get out of here?"

"If what you had is a panic attack, we can release you as soon as you feel strong enough to get up. If it was a heart attack, then we'll need to keep you here a bit longer to run a few more tests."

I looked at the Doc and laughed.

"I see. How about I just release myself when I'm feeling up to it. We'll go with that option," I said not giving her a choice.

"As you wish," she said with a look that said, 'You had a panic attack' written all across her face.

Fine. Whatever she needed to believe to allow me to get out of here.

"Could you send in my brother when you go," I said done with her.

"I'll send him right in," she said politely before showing herself out.

"What's the verdict," Lorenzo asked immediately entering.

"I think I was poisoned," I told him rolling the thought around in my mind.

"Kuroi! But how? The kiss!"

"The kiss," I concluded not giving any life to the other thing the doctor had suggested.

"He poisoned you with the kiss," Lorenzo concluded with a laugh. "Well, that would explain the look on your face after it happened."

"What do you mean?"

"You looked drugged. It was like you didn't even know where you were. Then you just took off."

"Yeah, that's probably what happened," I said slowly remembering the kiss.

Was that what happened? Things were coming back to me and any look I had on my face wasn't from a drug. I didn't go around kissing men. At least not in front of people who knew me. And doing what I did the way it happened and with him…

What was it about Kuroi? Was it his lips? His eyes? Oh right, the way he looked at me. It was like he slipped into me and became the puzzle piece that had been missing my entire life.

As a wolf, you grow up hearing a lot of talk about fated mates, people who the spirits have planned for you to be with. When you meet them, you're just supposed to know.

I never believed it, especially considering who got my dick hard. But the feeling I had looking into Kuroi's eyes made me wonder. I had never felt anything like it. Could that be what everyone was talking about?

Still, if I were poisoned, didn't it have to be from Kuroi's kiss? Could this have been the way he killed all of his lovers? The kiss of death? And wasn't it minutes after that I passed out?

"What are you gonna do about it?" Lorenzo asked bringing me back. "And, did you know Sato was planning on doing that? Marrying you two right there like that? It was nuts!"

"If I knew what he was planning, you think I would have gone there like that?"

"I don't know. For a moment there you did seem pretty into it," Lorenzo joked.

"Fuck no! That was a complete mind fuck what he did."

"Then, I don't get it. Why'd you go through with it? Why didn't you just stop it?"

That was a good question. Why didn't I? And that was when I remembered the look in Kuroi's eyes.

"I did it because our pack needed it," I lied.

Lorenzo threw his head back in admiration.

"You're a bigger man than me, Dante," my little brother said with a snort.

"And don't you fuckin' forget it," I joked.

"So, what are you gonna do now. You can't, like, live with him or anything, can you? He already tried to kill you once."

That was a good question. The living arrangements weren't something that Sato and I discussed. When I thought I was marrying Yuki, of course I imagined us living together. That would have been one of the benefits of the marriage. But now… shit.

What would living with Kuroi even be like? If he had tried to kill me, the fact that he failed would mean he would try again. How long could I sleep with one eye open?

And, what was with him wearing that dress? Yeah, he looked as hot as fuck in it. But if I was marrying a man, shouldn't he act like a man? I mean, having sex with a man is one thing. Guys have things that women don't. But, weren't men supposed to act like men?

Goddamn did he look hot in that dress, though. As male brides go, I must have had the hottest one to ever live. Unwrapping that gift would be the highlight of my life. I got hard just thinking about it.

"This is a marriage of convenience," I told Lorenzo. "The whole point of it is to show that our two organizations are one. Living together would be the point."

"Wow! My big brother just married a man," Lorenzo said with a mind-altered chuckle.

"Don't think that will stop me from kicking your ass if I have to," I said seriously.

"Believe me, it doesn't. If you're willing to do to that, what other crazy shit would you be willing to do? Granted, the man you married is likely to kill you in your sleep before the cock crows. But still."

"Don't you worry about me. I can take care of myself. The day I let some crazy twink come between me and what I want would be a cold day in hell."

"Twink?" Lorenzo asked surprised.

"That's what you call guys like Kuroi, right? I mean, that's what I've heard."

Lorenzo looked at me suspiciously. Shit! I had been married to Kuroi for one day and I was already slipping up. Maybe us living together would be too much. I had to rethink this.

Marriage was one thing. Hell, back in the old days, royalty would marry their cousins. But that didn't mean they lived together.

Yeah, that was what I was gonna do. I had already married him. There was nothing I could do about that. But I wouldn't be living with him. Not today. Not ever.

And if Sato ever asked why, I was going tell him because his slippery crow demon ass tricked me into marriage. My family's humiliation wasn't going further than that.

So, that was it. Kuroi, no matter what, would never move into my place. Ever. It was decided.

Chapter 5

Kuroi

What did a boy wear on the day he moved into his husband's house? So many options. Going through my closet, it was hard to choose.

"Let's see," I said fingering through my clothes. "Stella McCartney, Victoria Beckham? Armani would be a classic."

When I saw it, I knew. Alexander McQueen. Sleek and fierce. A girl had to make an impression on her first day. Would my new husband be there? Word was that he survived his little encounter with the deathies and was planning on heading home.

His new wife should be there to meet him, shouldn't he? Framed in Alexander McQueen, I'll greet him at the door, arms wide.

"It's decided, Alexander McQueen. Pack up the rest," I instructed my father's men who insisted on seeing me off.

Choosing a pair of black panties from my drawer, I slipped into them and clad myself in McQueen. Being the diva, I made my makeup Douyin. And completing the look, I chose a selection of feathers for my hair. Staring at myself in the mirror, I wanted him to see me. This look couldn't be wasted.

How many nights would we be able to share together before he was dead? He almost didn't last our wedding day. It would have been a shame too considering our kiss.

And let me tell you, that kiss… My tongue has been down a lot of straight men's throats. None of them made me feel like that. It was enough to give a girl hope.

Wasn't that how all marriages should start, full of hope and promise? I was a blushing bride, after all. And he, my dear Dante, was my big bad wolf.

Remembering the kiss again, I lost myself in the memory. How had he made me feel what I had? I had kissed him to unnerve him, to throw him off. Instead, I felt something.

Can you imagine me feeling something? Didn't feeling things go out of fashion in the 80s? Then again, retro chic was all the rage.

With a trunk of my essentials packed, I was loaded into my father's helicopter and flown to the city. Where did my betrothed live, I wondered? Landing on a downtown rooftop heliport, I was delighted to learn that it was in the city. I would have hated to have to scurry across town to get to my usual spots.

But now that I was a wife, perhaps my life would change. Would I still shut down Manhattan hot spots when I had wifely duties to fulfill? Perhaps instead, I would make him dinner every night losing myself in marital bliss. It would be me and my hubby together taking on the world.

My glorious fantasy ended when I arrived at his building looking like I stepped off a runway and the man at the building's desk tried to stop me from getting onto the elevator. Did I think about cutting his throat as he droned on about not being on the list? Of course. Why didn't I? Hello, Alexander McQueen!

Instead, my father's men broke a few of his fingers, took his key and ushered me up. The elevator opened to his apartment. Staring at the surprisingly tasteful décor, open space, and the Central Park view from the wall-length sliding glass doors, I didn't hate it.

"This will do," I said instructing the men to deposit my belongings in the living room and be off.

Once alone, I looked around at the place again. Immediately I saw how someone could be thrown from the balcony, deboned with the knives in the kitchen, and suffocated by any of the surprisingly large selection of throw pillows.

For exits, there was only one way out, the elevator. Buildings like this required a second exit for fire safety purposes. I'd have to figure out where that was.

Now here was the most important question. Did he have security cameras? Everyone under the age of 70 in his situation would. My father, as stuck in the old country as he was, had a camera in every room. Even mine.

When I ripped it down, his men would put it back up. It annoyed me until I discovered how much I enjoyed putting on a show. What made it better was that I didn't know who was watching or if anyone was watching at all. When I did see someone react differently to me after a particularly vigorous show, I waited until they were alone and marked them.

Nothing dramatic. I just gave them a small vertical cut under their left eye. In a few months, most people would barely notice the scar. But he would know it was there and would never forget. They never ruined my fantasies again after that.

So, did my husband have cameras tossed about? Slowly circling the space, I had to find out. The living room was spacious and cream-colored luxury, but camera-free. The kitchen was modern and looked surprisingly used, but still, there was nothing that recorded.

There were three bedrooms to choose from. Two were unoccupied guest rooms with king-sized beds but no cameras. And finally, his bedroom.

I got a little rush walking towards it. What would the bedroom of a man who kissed like that look like? The answer, it looked like sex.

There was a scent in the air. Was it his? It ripped through me raking my insides. A wave of heat billowed around my neck and spiraled down ending in my crotch. I was so hard it hurt.

More than that, there wasn't a camera in the place. Not just his bedroom, the entire flat. There could be only one reason for that. My hubby did things here that he didn't want recorded. And, that kiss…

Oh, I was going to fuck him. I would peel back Tom Ford, grab hold of what slithered out and suffocate it with my throat. I would become one of his secrets. Looking around at the space again, there was no question, this would work out quite nicely.

Hearing a chime that drew my attention to the elevator, I nearly choked. He was here. My husband had arrived. There was nothing that made me nervous but hearing it, my legs shook. Look at me, the virgin bride.

Searching for the bathroom, I rushed into it and checked my face. I wanted to look perfect. Well, maybe not perfect, but my makeup had to be flawless. Adjusting the creases on my suit, I gathered myself, walked back to the bedroom's door and presented myself to him.

I saw him before he saw me. I used the extra time to pose in the doorframe. This would be his first impression. The pose had to be dramatic. It was. And when he turned around and our eyes met, he froze.

It was like the moment before our kiss. I could see into him. He was rage and fire under molten a crust. At any moment he could explode. Feeling his fury rumble to the surface, I inhaled trembling and…

"Ugh," he grunted, turning away bored and heading toward the kitchen.

Wait? Did he just "ugh" me? Anger, lust, and madness exist and he… ignored me?

'Oh no!' I thought feeling a crackling in my head.

"Hello, your wife is home," I informed him giving him a second chance.

He glanced back at me again.

"All I see is a boy dressed up in women's clothes."

In an instant, I became blind with rage.

"This is Alexander McQueen!"

"I don't know who that is. And watch what you touch with all that makeup on. Either that or learn how to use a steam cleaner."

It was then that my mind floated to another place. It was there that I realized that I hadn't properly accessorized. I had thought bringing my knives too garish considering my form-fitting suit. So, sprinting across the room before my husband could open the fridge, I borrowed one of his from the butcher's block.

I would like to say that there was a reason I chose the one I did, but I was no longer the one in control. The spider demon had taken over and it seemed that she didn't feel the way I did about the new man in my life.

With a quick strike, she plunged the paring knife into the back of my husband's thigh. I didn't expect to hear him scream. He had to know it was coming, didn't he? Hadn't he practically begged for it?

Nonetheless, the poke woke him up. Still, I expected him to be quicker. Before he turned around, she had gotten him again. This time in the side. She did have a soft spot for him though, because she missed his organs. It was more of a Prince Albert entering one side and coming out the other.

It was only then that my hubby reacted. He was surprisingly fast for an old man. With the blade still in him, he reached back grabbing my neck. Bending me first, he tossed me across the room. My hubby was strong.

If that was his plan to stop the spider demon, he had another thing coming. No longer having the knife, she gathered herself and sprung back. Launching herself into the air, she landed on his neck. Holding on as he spun, her grip loosened when he backed her into the fridge.

He was definitely a strong one. And when he did it again with twice as much force, she let go her grip allowing him to take her by the throat, lift her over his head, and slam her onto the couch.

With his hands tightening around her neck, I saw something new in his eyes. He had chosen madness. It was glorious to see. The sight of it ushered the spider demon away and brought me back.

My hubby's hands were powerful. I was helpless. He could kill me with just the flick of his wrist. Would he?

As the darkness swallowed my sight, I wasn't sure. And just before my world blinked out, his face changed. Oh my god, my husband was shifting. Never having been with a wolf, I had only imagined what it would look like. Seeing him turn above me was incredible. Hoping to see more, I instead blacked out.

When I came to, things were much calmer. My husband was no longer choking the life out of me and I was no longer trying to kill him. I was instead desperately trying to catch my breath and he was shirtless and putting on his pants. More interesting than that, his spider bites were gone.

"Do you need help with that?" I asked, finding my voice.

"You're fuckin' nuts," he said barely looking at me.

"But honey, I'm your nuts," I crooned.

"Lucky me," he huffed sarcastically.

"I think you ruined my makeup," I admitted not wanting to see myself in the mirror.

"I think you stabbed me in the back."

"It was a love tap."

"You call that love."

"Do you think I couldn't find an artery?" I asked casually.

My husband paused sobering up.

"I don't know. Could you have?"

"There are six arteries that when cut would most-likely end in death, even for your kind. In the neck, the chest, the collar, the arm, the pelvis, and oh yeah, four inches down from the bite in your thigh."

"Shit!" he cooed.

"Like I said, a love tap," I told him before he got up, headed to his room and locked the door behind him.

This was going to make performing my wifely duties on our wedding night a challenge. It looks like I got 'the talk' for nothing.

Holding out hope that he just needed to straighten his room before inviting me in, I got comfortable on the couch and waited for him to return. I stared at his door all night. He never came out. Still there and awake as the sun peeked in through the skyscrapers, I eventually heard his door crack.

Sitting up, I was sure I looked a mess. I should have cleaned myself up. I was wearing yesterday's makeup and a wrinkled suit. What was I thinking? This was no way to keep a man.

Putting my skank aside, I put my hands in my lap and made myself the vision of elegance. There was no way he would be able to resist this lady, but somehow he did. Exiting his room fully dressed, he barely looked at me. When he did in response to my eagerness, he held up a finger freezing me.

I'll be honest, I didn't know how to react to that. By the time I had decided, he was already entering the elevator.

"Would you like me to make you some coffee?" I asked a closing elevator door.

The truth was that I had no idea how to make coffee. Coffee was one of those things that had appeared fully formed in mugs or cups. But it couldn't be that hard to figure out, could it?

Suspecting my love was gone for the day, I slumped in my seat and lowered my head into my hands. Feeling them slide, I remembered how I looked. Examining my hands, they were caked with foundation. I had to clean myself off.

To do that I considered heading to Dante's bathroom. I thought better of it. It wasn't because he didn't want me there. I just didn't want to leave it a mess. So, choosing one of the guest bedroom's bathrooms, I gathered my supplies.

Clean, I next entered the shower. Naked to the world, the reality of my life snuck in. Faced with it, I didn't like the way it looked. Luckily, the thought didn't stay long. And exiting the shower without getting dressed. I took another tour of my new home which ended with me crawling into his bed.

It was definitely his musk that I smelled. It was intoxicating. Wrapping my arms around his pillow and pulling it to me, I tried to wrap my legs around it. I needed him to touch me. I yearned to feel his large hand grab my ass and make it his.

Lying there a bitch in heat, there was no relief except sleep. I had been awake all night waiting for him to come to me. He never had. He had to be taught a lesson for that. I was his wife, after all. That was no way to be treated.

However, waking up feeling rested, revenge was no longer on my mind. Was it June Cleaver who said that you catch more flies with honey? Or, did she say that the way to a man's heart was through his stomach?

Either way, I needed to take a different approach. I would be the perfect wife. Wearing pearls and high heels, I would bake a casserole. It couldn't be that hard, could it? I just had to call the chef, tell them what I wanted, and it was done.

More pressing than the meal was the outfit I would wear. I had the perfect pearls. Unfortunately, they were back at my father's house. And the idea of leaving this place to get it didn't sit right with me.

If I left, would I be able to get back in? Of course, I would. I was Dante's wife, after all. When I returned he would be happy to see me.

Still, entering the elevator felt like a one way trip.

"Yuki, can you do me a favor?" I asked over the phone.

When Yuki arrived, it was with more than just my pearls.

"I have a gift for you," she said with one of her delicate smiles.

"A wedding gift?" I said taking the box.

Unwrapping it, what I found brought a smile to my face. It was couture and very me.

"I love it!" I told her immediately missing my sister.

"How was your first night?" she asked with sadness in her eyes.

"As a married woman? Everything I dreamed of," I said continuing the fantasy.

Sitting next to me Yuki put her hand on my thigh.

"Kuroi, I'm sorry Father did this to you."

"No, it's okay. I really think this might be a good thing."

Yuki met my eyes.

"Seriously, Yuki. Things have started off a little rocky, but he might be the one," I said trying to look past evidence to the contrary.

Yuki slowly scanned the room. All of my stuff still sat just inside the living room. The kitchen looked like the scene of a knife fight. And there were drops of blood on the area rug.

When her gaze returned to me, I lowered my eyes. With an elegance that I could only pretend to have, Yuki straightened her spine and turned to me.

"Do you know why father named you Kuroi?" she asked as if pouring alcohol into an open wound.

"I think everyone knows why he named me that," I said as my thumb tried one last time to rub the darkness off of me.

"It wasn't because of your dark skin," she said to my surprise. "It was to mark you as the dark stain on his honor. Father could not resist your mother's power of seduction. And you were the price he paid for his moment of weakness."

I cringed hearing what I had always suspected but had never wanted to hear spoken.

"He lost everything for keeping you. There were those who had told him to toss you into the ocean. Even our brothers had told him this. But he didn't. He kept you. And he knew for you to survive, you would need to learn your place.

"But you were stubborn. Like petrified bamboo, you would not bend. That is why he made you kagema. It was to teach you your place. It was to help you."

Yuki's words cut through me leaving me raw and bare. No one had ever told me, but my father said enough for me to figure what my mother was.

She was a succubus who worked as a prostitute. That made me a half breed. That meant I could inherit my father's curse or my mother's powers of seduction. Considering that lovers keep dying, it's clear which one I got.

"What are you telling me to do?" I asked again becoming the 14-year-old ripped from my home.

"To grow in the field, bamboo must bend."

"You're saying I should submit? To who? My husband? Father?"

"You must bend," my submissive sister repeated.

Was my sister right? In our world, she had certainly thrived. With her gentle demeanor and softened words, she had become Father's favorite. There was nothing he wouldn't do for her. She had our father wrapped around her finger.

Was there power in submission? Could I have that power? Would that power give me Dante? As what? My lover? My love? Could anyone love a black stain like me?

Words between Yuki and me were no longer necessary. Silence overtook us. Instead of arguing with her, I tried something new. I bent. Mostly it was to join her as she picked up after my husband and my knife fight. It wasn't so bad.

Could I submit to the extent my sister had? Probably not. Yuki had made it an art form. In every way she was a proper Japanese. And what was I?

No matter. It wasn't what I was. It was what I could become. I would become my sister.

I would lower my eyes when men spoke. I would bow in the presence of my elders. And I would be the perfect wife for a man like Dante Ricci, my husband and superior.

Chapter 6

Dante

Turning my family's organization into a legitimate set of businesses has its perks. One is that I get to go into an office. That's particularly good right now because it gets me away from the crazy fuck I married.

Don't get me wrong, seeing Kuroi in that suit with his makeup was almost more than I could take. It took me everything I had to prevent my wolf from fucking him until I couldn't see straight. The man has a way of making me feel things I know I shouldn't. It was like he had some type of power over me.

But it's hard to imagine us having any type of life together while dodging his stabs. I've got to hand it to him, the man is quick. Even with my enhanced alpha strength, I couldn't just hold him off to keep him away from me. He made me work for it. I had to let my wolf out to keep him from killing me.

The crazy thing is that I don't think he was trying to kill me. He was right, there were a number of arteries he could have gone after if he was hoping to end my life. That confuses the fuck out of me because if he was trying to kill me with a poisonous kiss at our wedding, why would he intentionally miss the killing blow when he had another opportunity?

It didn't make sense. Of course, nothing made sense with that crazy fucker. One thing for certain was that I couldn't turn my back on him. I was also going to have to pay Sato's men a visit for what they did to Franko, the attendant at my building. The man has a family and needs to make a living.

He can't come into work every day scared that doing his job will get his fingers broken. Now, not only do I have to pay his hospital bills and for his time off from work to get him to come back, but his Christmas tip has to be as much as a small car. Christ, how much will being married to Kuroi cost me?

"I heard Sato's men attacked your doorman last night," Matteo said when I entered my office to find him there.

I paused quickly assessing what was going on. I hadn't had the chance to tell the rest of my family about the wedding. I was too busy recovering from an attempt on my life.

And last night after leaving the hospital, I was preoccupied with how I was going to break it to Sato that Kuroi and I wouldn't be living together. That was, of course, before I got home to find him already there and looking like the most fuckable thing I've ever seen.

"There was an incident. I'm taking care of it," I informed my brother before heading to my desk. "What are you doing here?"

"Pa sent me to check on you. He didn't have enough time to see you at the hospital," Matteo said playing the subtle game with a level of skill I didn't think he had.

"There was no need to stop by. It was a brief stay."

"A brief stay because you ran that beautiful car of yours into a tree. What possessed you to do that? The Dante I knew would need to get shot to do something like that."

Hearing his reference to getting shot, I looked up at Matteo. Was this a new level to his subtle game?

"Why'd you say that?" I asked suspiciously.

"Say what?"

"That I would need to get shot to crash my car."

"Because you would. You loved that car. You acted like you would take a bullet for that car," he explained as I looked for any hint that he might have been behind the neck pinch I felt before I crashed.

"I didn't love the car that much," I told him when I didn't spot anything.

"So, what happened?"

Not liking where his questioning was going, I settled at my desk and began my day.

"What happened was that I crashed."

"But why? We had someone check in on the doctor but she wasn't saying."

"We?"

"Yeah, you know, Pa and me."

"So it's you and Pa now. After everything he put the both of us through, that's still where your loyalty lies? After all of the cleaning up I've had to do with your messes?"

"Hey, I never asked you to do the things you've done," he said defensively.

"You never had to. That's what it means to be a pack. We look after each other. It would be good for you to remember that."

"I remember that," Matteo said backing down a little.

"Good," I said turning my attention to my computer hoping he would see himself out.

"But, speaking of cleaning up my mess. Pa and me were wondering what happened with that idea you had about marrying one of Sato's people?"

Did he know? He had to know something. If they knew what hospital I was in, it wouldn't be hard for them to figure out what else is near there and then piece together why I was there.

Shit! I was going to have to tell everyone. And there was no way I was gonna avoid telling them that the head of the Ricci pack had just married a man.

"Yeah, it's been settled," I said casually.

"How? When did this happen?"

"Yesterday. There was a small ceremony at Sato's place."

The silence that drew out made me look up. Matteo was more than just stunned, he was white-faced.

"What do you mean there was a small ceremony at Sato's place?"

"I took care of it."

"You took care of it as in, you're now a married man?"

"Yeah. I took care of it," I said trying to raise my voice to make it seem like he was the idiot for making me repeat myself, but my heart wasn't in it.

"So, my big brother, and the alpha of the Ricci pack, got married with no one from the pack there?"

"Of course not. Lorenzo was there."

Matteo, who had gotten up to talk to me across my desk, flopped down into a chair. He pulled on his face like his head was spinning.

"What? It's not a big deal. There was a problem you caused, and like usual, I took care of it. What's new about that?"

"What's new is that you got fuckin' married."

"Yeah," I confirmed starting to get a little confused regarding what we were talking about.

"My big brother, who I always imagined standing by his side on his big day, got married and the only one there was Lorenzo?"

"Matteo, it's not a big deal."

"Not a big deal? Dante, Ricci wolves only get married once. You hear me? Once! And now, the person I admire more than anyone in this world is married, and I wasn't there to bear witness to it?"

"Bear witness to it? What are you talking about, Matteo. It's not a big deal."

Staring at Matteo, I saw his eyes get glassy. What was going on? I had once watched him nearly beat a man to death. I had watched our father almost beat him to death. And not even then did he cry. I was starting to think that I might have done something wrong.

"Okay," Matteo said pulling himself together. "Then can you at least tell me who my new sister is?"

My chest tightened like a drum. His new sister? The idea that I could be with a man wasn't even imaginable to him. I didn't know if I could do this.

"It's a little more complicated than that."

"More complicated? How can it be more complicated?"

There was no way of escaping this, especially with my new husband having moved in with me. I glanced down at the papers on my desk not able to meet his eyes.

"Look, what you did was bad. I had to stop a war. Who knows how many people would end up dead if I didn't make this move."

"What are you saying?"

"What I'm saying is that I didn't marry a she. It's a he."

Shock overwhelmed my brother. Every second that went by without him speaking made my wolf nervous.

"What are you thinking, Matteo?" I asked wondering if I was gonna have to get physical.

"I…"

"You what?"

"I don't understand," he said looking genuinely confused.

"Look, it turns out that Yuki wasn't available. I think she was promised to someone else or some shit. And since we needed to make this work, the only option was Kuroi."

Matteo flinched in surprise. "Kuroi? You mean, the fuckin' spider demon? What the fuck, Dante?"

"Don't believe that spider demon bullshit. I've met him. He's a perfectly reasonable guy."

As proof, I could add that he didn't even cut an artery when he stabbed me multiple times the night before.

"Reasonable guy? Dante, haven't you heard? That guy's a psycho! Yeah, he's not bad to look at if you're into that sort of thing." Matteo paused. "Dante, are you into that sort of thing?"

Fuck! That was a point-blank question. I had managed to avoid this type of question my whole life. Marry one man and the shit just hits the fan.

"You know me, right, Matteo? You know me. I am willing to do whatever it takes to protect our pack. We need this connection."

"We don't need it that much."

"Matteo, we need it! You don't know what type of shit your acting out put us in!"

"You being forced to marry someone you don't want to would never be worth it. It was one thing when I thought it was Yuki. I could see the two of you really working together. But Kuroi? The guy's a psycho. Nothing is worth that. I mean, if you're not into it," he said suggestively.

"What's done is done. Do you hear me? And secondly, now that he is my husband, I can't have you goin' around disparaging him like that. Do you hear me? You disrespect him, you're disrespecting me."

Matteo looked at me shocked.

"I said, do you hear me!"

"Yeah, of course. Whatever, Dante," my brother said looking very confused.

We both stared at each other in silence for a moment. I didn't know what he was thinking but I had gotten it out.

"Is this gonna be a problem?" I asked my shell-shocked brother.

"Of course not, Dante. No problem."

"Good. Is there anything else?"

"One thing. How are you planning on breaking this to Pa? I mean, you know me, I'm open minded. But he isn't exactly from our school of thought."

Our school of thought? What exactly was Matteo saying to me?

"I assume that you're gonna run back to him with this?"

"I'm hoping I don't have to?"

"You don't have to do shit."

"Dante, you married a fuckin' man! No disrespect for it. But, he's gonna find out."

Matteo was right. He couldn't be blindsided with this. Coming from the wrong person, he was likely to shift and kill them for telling him.

I grabbed the spot on my side where Kuroi had stabbed me. The wound had healed after I had shifted, but I could still feel it. Sometimes it took a shifters brain time to catch up to the instant healing that came with a shift.

"You alright?"

"I'm fine. Seat belts keep you alive, but…" I said implying that my discomfort came from that.

"Wait. Did your accident have anything to do with getting married at Sato's place yesterday?"

How did I explain that?

"It happened when I was driving away."

He looked at me confused.

"So, what happened to Lorenzo? Didn't you say he was there with you?"

"Not when I was heading out."

"Why wasn't he with you when you were heading out?"

"I needed to go out and get some fuckin' air. Do you have a problem with that?"

Matteo backed off.

"I don't have a problem with it. I'm just trying to understand what happened. You know Pa is gonna ask me about this."

"Just tell him, what you know. I don't have any secrets."

"Are you sure about that?" he asked me cutting to the heart of things.

"Look. Tell him what you gotta tell him. I have nothin' to hide. I did what I had to do. Now it's done."

"You know Ma's gonna want to meet him, right? She's gonna expect you to bring him by for Sunday dinner. There's no way you're gonna escape that."

Oh fuck. He was right. No matter what Pa thought about this, Ma was gonna welcome him into the pack. She's gonna want to have him over and she'll expect him to act like a part of the family.

How was I gonna bring my crazy new dress-wearing husband to one of our off-the-rail family dinners? If anyone says anything about his dresses, someone could end up dead.

"You keep reachin' for your side. Are you sure you're okay, Dante?"

"I'm fine." I told him starting to wonder if what I had was a panic attack. Or maybe the walls really were closing in on me.

"Listen, I gotta get to work. Is there anything else you need from me?"

"Yeah, I need you to break this news to Pa so I don't have to."

"Noted."

"And I need you to reassure me that this whole thing isn't gonna blow up in your face."

"Everything's under control."

"I hope it is," Matteo said with true concern. Turning to go, he said, "Maybe you, me, and your new husband should go out for a test run before you introduce him to the rest of the pack. You know…"

"…Because we can't be sure if the rest of the pack thinks like us?"

"Exactly."

"I'll think about it," I told him turning my focus to my computer monitor.

When Matteo closed the door behind him, I looked up. The air refilled my lungs like a wind tunnel. Everything about our conversation was unexpected. Out of everyone, I thought Matteo would take me being with a man the worst. He wasn't exactly known for thoughtful contemplation.

But he had said that no one else could be trusted to think like us. What exactly did that mean? How did we think?

I've never known my pretty boy brother and I to think alike about anything. But he definitely meant something by it. The question was, what?

Another question was, how was I going to break it to our father that I had married Sato's son? Yet another question was, would Kuroi kill me before I got the opportunity?

The guy really was insane. Nice to look at, like Matteo had said, but completely insane. He stabbed me during our first night together. For what?

Maybe I just needed to give him some space. This couldn't have been his idea to get married. Maybe if I gave him a wide berth, he'll get used to things and he wouldn't be so stabby next time. Or maybe I should just hide the knives.

How the fuck did I get myself into this? Fuckin' Matteo!

Having come up with a vague outline for how I was going to handle Kuroi moving forward, I turned my attention to the other matters at hand. First off, someone had tried to kill me. Having failed, they were going to try again.

Secondly, I couldn't trust our father to just accept me leading the pack. He was going to try something. Once he found out about Kuroi, it was just a matter of when.

Touching base with Lorenzo about what I thought was going on, I left out the part about my new husband trying to turn me into a shish kabab. He suspected that it was Kuroi behind my passing out before the crash. Leaving out that Kuroi had purposefully not killed me, made it hard to explain why I had my doubts about that.

"He kissed you, minutes later, you crashed," he told me over lunch.

"If he wanted me dead, he could've killed me while I slept," I said even though I didn't sleep a wink last night.

"Wait, how could he? Does he even know where you live?"

"Of course he does. He moved in."

Lorenzo froze about to shove a piece of lettuce into his mouth.

"I thought you said you two would live separately?"

"Don't go puttin' words in my mouth," I said playing off anything I might or might not have said.

"I'm not tryin' to put words in your mouth. I just thought you said it."

"Well, I didn't."

I was sure that I thought it. And that might have been the plan. But, I wasn't sure that the words came out of my mouth.

"Anyway, how was your first night as a married man? Everything nice and consummated?" he joked.

"That will be the day," I replied way more turned on by the thought of it than I was gonna let on.

"So, when am I going to meet my new brother?"

"What is with everybody being in a rush to meet him?"

"Everybody?"

"You, Matteo."

"Matteo knows? What'd he say?" Lorenzo asked weirdly interested.

"You know our brother."

"Huh," Lorenzo huffed before returning to his lunch.

"He did say something interesting, though. He said that Ma was gonna expect me to bring him by for dinner."

"Ha! That is a dinner I would come for," he said amused.

"Yeah. Imagine that?"

"There's no imagining. He's right. Ma's gonna make you do that," he said casually.

"You think?"

"I know."

"Huh," I said thinking about that. "Matteo did say something else."

"He was just full of interesting thoughts today."

"Yeah. He said that maybe I should invite Kuroi to have dinner with someone from the family first. You know, to make sure nothing goes wrong."

"What could go wrong?" Lorenzo said with a laugh.

"Exactly. So, what do you think?"

"What? With me? I would love it. It'll also give me a chance to figure out if he's the one who tried to kill you."

"I don't think he's trying to kill me," I said dismissively.

Lorenzo looked up at me amused.

"Who would have thought, Dante Ricci, blinded by a pretty face? Ha!"

I didn't respond. First off, my wolf didn't like my brothers thinking they could comment on my husband's looks like that. Let's have some respect. Bat-shit crazy or not, he was still my husband. They were gonna have to understand that.

Second, they weren't wrong. I could feel a blind spot developing for Kuroi. Anyone else do to me what he did and I would have ended their life right there. I wouldn't have just choke the life out of them, I would have tossed them off my balcony.

It was more than needing things to work out between our two families that kept me from killing him. The man was a live wire that I wanted to touch.

Drawing out things at work as long as possible, eventually I headed home. Driving in my rental, I could feel my wolf wanting to come out. He got like this whenever I was nervous. But I didn't get nervous. So, I didn't know why he was acting this way.

Parking and heading into the lobby, I was reminded what I was walking into by Franko's replacement.

"Good evening, Mr. Ricci," he said opening the elevator for me.

"Evening."

When the elevator door closed behind me, I forcefully inhaled. I couldn't breathe. I never felt like this. What was going on?

Hearing the bing as the door opened, I realized that whatever I was feeling was a little too much. I needed to get into my room as fast as I could and come up with a way to handle things.

Stepping out of the elevator, I instinctually looked around.

"Hey Honey, you're home!" my husband said from the kitchen.

I knew I should have kept going, but I couldn't. The man was wearing a 1950s checkboard dress full with pearls, an apron, and a dish of casserole in his hands.

"What's on your face?" I said before I could stop myself.

"What do you mean?" He said smiling at me in full white face like one of those Kabuki performers.

I laughed. Maybe it wasn't a laugh. It might have been more of a dismissive humph. In either case, it was then that my legs started moving and I continued to my room.

You would think, as skinny as he was, my new husband wouldn't be able to throw a casserole dish like he did. But he could. And his aim was spot on.

Not only did he manage to hit me with it from across the room. But the dish caught me on the one spot that could drop a person if caught exactly right. I was on the ground before I knew it.

Lying defenselessly, I half expected to be turned into Swiss cheese. Not this time. This time, he pulled the apron strap from over his head and wrapped it around my throat. You had to give him points for improvisation.

I mean, someone had to. I was too busy trying to stay alive. If I didn't get up, I was sure that I was never going to again. This time he really was trying to kill me. At least I wouldn't have to listen to my father say he told me so. Or listen to Ma tell Kuroi embarrassing stories about my childhood.

Strangely, it was the thought of Kuroi sitting in my childhood living room hearing stories about me from Ma that kept me from giving up. I think there was some part of me that wanted that.

Before this moment, I could never have imagined a husband truly being a part of my life. But that was what I wanted. It had always been what I wanted. I had never let myself acknowledge it before, but that was the version of my life that was worth fighting for.

With a new focus, I reached behind me and grabbed the apron string. Pulling it just enough, I was able to twist throwing him off balance. With the apron string loosening more, I yanked him towards me, grabbed his dress, and tossed him over my head.

Rolling forward, he didn't stop until he was again on his feet. But he was faced the other way. This was my chance. Struggling for air, I shot to my feet and dove for his waist.

The man wasn't a spider, he was a cat. Twisting around as I caught him, I half expected to feel a knife sever the carotid artery in my neck.

Alive for another second, I let instincts take over. Disabling him, I spun and threw his shoulder onto the ground. It startled him. It was enough for me to wrap my large hands around his skull. Knowing this was life or death, I slammed it against the floor.

That stunned him. Rolling on top of him, I wrapped my hands around his throat and tightened my grip. I could see the life slip out of him. His was such a beautiful face. The sharp cheekbones, prominent eyebrows, silky brown complexion. What was I doing?

Catching myself as I saw blood below his nose, I eased back without letting go. Where was he bleeding? Even now my desire to protect him was strong.

'Oh shit, it's coming from me. And it's gushing.'

It looked like Kuroi didn't need to strangle me. He had opened a gash big enough on my head that given enough time, I would bleed out.

"You crazy fuck," I said letting him go and grabbing my skull.

"How would you know?" he coughed out.

"What?" I asked confused if he was flirting with me or questioning my judgment.

Not taking my eyes off of him, I stumbled to my feet and applied pressure to my head waiting for the elevator. When it arrived, I backed in, stared into his intense eyes, and waited for the doors to close.

Safe, I knew what I had to do. I either needed to shift or get help. Considering how much blood I was losing, shifting wouldn't be an automatic fix. I was bleeding a lot. And if the shifting didn't fully heal me, I would be a bleeding wolf with nowhere to go and no way to get there.

Feeling weaker with every passing second, I decided the better plan would be to get help. I couldn't stick around here because if my psycho husband decided to take a second whack at me, there would be nothing I could do but die.

"Mr. Ricci, are you alright?" the lobby attendant asked as I rushed past him.

"I'm fine."

"Do you need me call someone?"

"No!" I ordered making sure he saw the look in my eyes.

It worked. At least I hoped it did. Looking down, my clothes were beginning to look like I went to prom in a horror movie. I had to get out of here. I needed to get into my car and get to the one place I knew I would be safe.

Approaching Lorenzo's apartment, I found a spot on the sidewalk to park and shut off the engine. I'm not gonna lie to you. I probably shouldn't have made it. I was seeing double of everything on the drive over and it was a miracle that I kept choosing the right car to ignore.

Pulling out my phone I found Lorenzo's name and called.

"What's up, Dante?" Lorenzo asked a little confused.

"I'm downstairs. Bring your kit. Someone got me good."

"Coming down now," he said again proving that he was the one person I could count on.

Feeling my vision dip in and out, it felt like forever before I saw my brother and my car door opened.

"Shit! What happened?" he asked reaching for my head instead of waiting for an answer.

"I fell," I mumbled.

"Right," he chuckled. "And how's married life?"

"Peachy," I replied before the sting of alcohol sent shockwaves across my face.

"Someone did get you good," he confirmed. "Remind me to go for the head next time I need to take someone out. I'm surprised you even made it here."

After what felt like five stitches, he handed me a meal replacement drink and straw, closed my door and got into the passenger seat. To my relief, he didn't ask me any questions. At least, not until I had gotten half of my drink down.

"You're not planning on going home, are you?"

"Why not? I told you, I fell."

"Into what? A bat?"

"It was a casserole dish, actually. My loving husband had just made me dinner."

Lorenzo looked at me not knowing what to believe.

"You want to come up?" he asked unsure what else to say.

"I might need a minute before I can shift again. After that I'll head home," I told him embarrassed.

"Get out," he said before switching seats with me and driving my car into his building's underground parking lot.

Giving me another second before we got out of the car, I saw him texting someone.

"You're gonna keep this shit between us, right?" I said in a way that let him know I was serious.

"What are you, insane? Of course," he said continuing to text.

I let it go and eventually I could see straight for long enough to get out of the car and head to the elevator. Getting off on his floor, I saw a guy heading towards us in the hallway. Lorenzo was going to have to handle this because I couldn't. I was the one covered in blood. I was in no position to threaten anyone into silence.

To my surprise, Lorenzo didn't handle it. There was no need. The man didn't look at either of us. What made it stranger was that Lorenzo didn't look at him. It was like I was seeing someone who wasn't there. He was, though. There was no doubt about that.

"Go clean up. I'll bring you some clothes," he told me as we entered his apartment.

With a reminder for which door was the bathroom, I headed in and slumped onto the basin. Looking up into the mirror, I wondered how I was still alive. My face was mostly blood. It looked like I had bathed in the shit.

How the fuck did I get myself into this? Was Kuroi really out to kill me? I couldn't tell if he was doing a piss poor job of it or if he was toying with me.

And what did "How would you know?" mean? How did I know he was a crazy fuck? Because he threw a casserole dish at me. Or, was he suggesting something about what would happen if we had sex? How crazy good could fucking him be?

"I got these," Lorenzo said bringing me back to the present.

I looked at the t-shirt and sweatpants in his hand. Was he kidding?

"It's the only thing I have that would fit you."

He was probably right. Not only was he shorter than my six foot four inches, he didn't have my build.

"Sit down. I'll do it," he insisted when he saw that I was gripping onto the basin for dear life.

I slowly straightened my back and unbuttoned my shirt. When I took too long, he took over and pulled my shirt down past my shoulders. I looked away embarrassed that I couldn't do this myself.

Even so, having Lorenzo clean me off felt familiar. Growing up, there were five of us, but it was more like there was me, and then there was Matteo, Giovanni, and Marco. Giovanni and Marco were too young to know any better, but Matteo used that to his advantage. The three of them would ambush me usually with Matteo hitting me in the head with one of the younger one's toys.

Just because it was made for kids didn't mean it couldn't draw blood. When I wasn't knocked unconscious, Matteo would immediately pay for it. But when I would gush like I did tonight, it was in everyone's best interest that I be patched up as quickly as possible.

That was when Lorenzo stepped in. Lorenzo sewed his first butterfly stitch when he was ten. We all considered him neutral territory. It allowed him to get good at it. Because if Matteo drew blood, it was just a matter of time before I gave Matteo a limp for a month. It was amazing how that boy never learned his lesson. He has a thick head to this day.

All of that was before any of us could shift, of course. Once our wolves came out, we could heal most injuries by shifting. It was only on rare occasions that shifting wasn't enough. When it wasn't, Lorenzo would again take care us so Pa didn't find out.

"I have Chinese if you're still hungry," he told me as he finished up.

"I could eat," I told him knowing I still wasn't strong enough to shift.

Changing into Lorenzo's clothes, I joined him at the table.

"Did I interrupt something?" I asked noticing how put together the things on the table were.

"What could you interrupt?"

I stared at my black box of a brother realizing he wasn't gonna give anything up. So instead I joined him at the table and dug in. Food was just what I needed. I ate until I couldn't move.

"You can stay in the spare room."

"I don't need to stay in your spare room," I said feeling pissed off at his suggestion. What did he think, that I couldn't take care of myself?

"Dante," he said looking at me with sympathy, "I know why you did it. And it's commendable. You're doing more for Matteo than I would. But, the man you married is trying to kill you."

"He's not."

"You've been married to him for three days. In those days, how many times have you had to shift to heal?"

"Hey, one of those times was from a car accident."

"… Five minutes after marrying the man known as the spider demon because everyone he's with dies from a heart attack. I can't remember, what caused you to run into that tree, again?"

Lorenzo was being an asshole about it, but he wasn't wrong. Unless it was a panic attack that caused me to hit that tree, I had to accept that it had to do with Kuroi's kiss. That made it three injuries and two times that I had had to shift.

But, if Kuroi was trying to kill me, why hadn't he just done it that first night. He had a knife. He knew where to aim it. Why hadn't he tried to break into my room when I was supposed to be asleep and finish me off?

Even tonight. Who makes a casserole and tries to murder someone with the dish? There has got to be more to what's going on than him being a raving maniac with impeccable fashion sense.

Speaking of, why was he dressed like that when I got home? I've never had a fetish. But that man was definitely doing something to me. If he ever stopped trying to kill me, I would do incredibly dirty things to him.

"Did you hear me, Dante? You can't go home. I need more time before I take over the pack. So, I need you alive a little longer."

My eyes locked on him giving him a death stare. He wasn't joking. He also wasn't backing down from what he said.

I could respect that. Lorenzo knew what he wanted and didn't try to hide it. He wanted my job but wasn't willing to kill me for it. He should have that type of ambition. I could work with that.

He didn't have what was needed to lead a pack. Neither he nor Matteo did. Combine the two and they would be a dangerous force. But running a pack was more than just snarling when someone threatened your dominance. It required letting people inside.

It might frustrate the hell out of you like Matteo frustrated me. But it was what was necessary. Lorenzo couldn't do that.

And what Matteo needed was some of Lorenzo's foresight. Hell, Matteo just needed not to act on whatever random thought went through his head. Not even our father ran the pack that way and we had barely survived it.

"You're my brother. Don't make me have to put you in the ground," I warned him.

"You think you could if you tried?" he asked with a smile.

What did he mean by that? Of course I could. Was he better at building allies than I gave him credit for?

"Don't make me have to try," I said staring him in the eyes.

"You can sleep in the spare room," he replied leaving the table and heading to his room.

I had to watch Lorenzo. He was the last person I would expect to betray me. But that made him the most dangerous.

Sitting for a while longer, I eventually took Lorenzo up on his offer and retired to his spare room. In spite of Lorenzo's open challenge, I slept well that night. I hadn't gotten any sleep the night before, so I needed it.

And once I was up the next morning, I shifted and felt as good as new.

Returning to my place a little after sunrise, I found Kuroi sleeping in my bed. I was quiet so I didn't think I had woken him. That allowed me to stare at my new husband, the beautiful boy in my bed.

He slept so peacefully under my sheets. I couldn't help but like that. At the same time, why hadn't he slept in the spare room?

How amazing would it be if I was in that bed with him? He would fit so comfortably in my arms. I could hold him and protect him from the world if he let me. But maybe I was thinking about this wrong.

I hadn't been in this position before. There had been guys in my bed but none of them were allowed to spend the night. Kuroi looked like he belonged there. But maybe I was projecting what I wanted onto a man who was lying in wait to kill me.

Closing my eyes and shaking the thought out of my head, I headed for my bathroom and began my day. As I stood under the shower, I could feel every phantom pain. Maybe Kuroi was a spider demon after all. Supernatural attacks were known to linger.

Out of the shower and getting dressed, the opening bathroom door grabbed my attention. Staring past my changing room, our eyes met. Kuroi was wearing nothing but boxer briefs. For the first time I was seeing him. No crazy outfit or face paint. Just him. All of him. My wolf liked what I saw.

"Let me help you," he said in a soft voice headed towards me.

I quickly assessed the weapons he could use between where he was and where I was as well as the placement of my gun. Turns out I didn't need any of them. The only thing he reached for was my shirt. Feeling his body heat wash over me, I could smell his faint scent as he pulled the shirt over my shoulders. I began to tell him that I didn't need his help, but I stopped enjoying how close he was to me.

With my shirt on, he buttoned me up. I couldn't tell if he saw that my wounds were gone. If he did, he didn't react to it. He simply tucked my shirt into my pants and searched my closet for a jacket. Retrieving one, he handed it to me.

"I don't need it," I told him never wearing a jacket to the office.

"You would look good in it," he said, shaking it in front of me.

I couldn't refuse him. Staring into his mesmerizing eyes, all I could do was give him what he wanted.

Taking the jacket, I stuck my arm in a sleeve. Helping me with the other, he next turned me towards the full length mirror. Standing behind me he stared at me in it. Liking what he saw, he smiled.

"Better?"

"Yeah, better," I replied referring to everything that was going on.

"Would you like me to make you some breakfast?"

"You make breakfast?" I asked him surprised.

"I have a phone," he joked.

I laughed, but only briefly. I hadn't forgotten how he had responded the last time I had laughed at him. Remembering that, I walked out of his hands and headed for the door.

"I have to go," I said hurrying out.

"See you tonight?" He said leaning against the doorway of my bedroom.

I flinched.

What did that mean? Sure, he was being nice this morning but wasn't he nice to me yesterday morning as well. What injury would I need to shift to heal tonight?

This was ridiculous. His mood swings were out of control. Yeah, I probably hadn't reacted in the best way when I saw him last night. But his response had been above and beyond. If he were anyone else, he would be dead right now.

The problem was that he wasn't anyone else. He was Kuroi Sato, my husband. That fact alone meant I didn't have the same options. I was defenseless against him. And if I didn't get control of things before he realized it, I was in trouble.

Getting into my car, I dialed the only person I could trust.

"Lorenzo, meet me in my office in an hour."

"I'll be there," he agreed sounding like he knew what it was about.

Staring out at the city from my office window, Lorenzo entered all business.

"You're right. I have a problem at home and I need your help," I admitted, as hard as it was to say.

"You want me to take care of him?"

Just hearing him say it sent me into a fury.

"Don't you ever fuckin' say those words again."

Lorenzo didn't flinch. Instead, he tilted his head like a curious puppy.

"Then why did you ask me here?"

"I need your brain. I need a way to solve this."

"So, you want me to get him to kill you slower?"

"I told you. I don't think he's trying to kill me."

He laughed.

"I'm serious."

Frustrated, he replied, "You kissed him and then immediately drove your car into a tree. Give me an alternative explanation for that."

I thought about what the doctor said about me having a panic attack.

"I felt something on my neck."

"What?"

"Yeah. Right before I passed out."

"What did you feel?"

"It felt like someone shot me." I touched the spot letting him see it, "But even before I shifted, there was no wound."

"What feels like a gunshot but doesn't leave a wound?" Lorenzo thought about it seriously. "Have you ever been hit by a Taser?"

"No. What does it feel like?" I asked intrigued.

"Like you've been shot."

"But I was driving when I felt it."

"How fast were you going?"

"You saw the wreck. Pretty fast."

Lorenzo's head bobbled considering it.

"There are other things."

"Like what?"

"Like what you use to bring down a wolf."

"Like a tranquilizer gun."

"Possibly. It would take a hell of a shot, though."

"Who do we know that could make a shot like that?"

As soon as I asked, Lorenzo and I thought about the same person. I could tell by the way he looked at me. Matteo made a lot of impulsive decisions. But give him time and a sharpshooter rifle and what's in his sights is the only thing that exists. Through an open window traveling at 40 miles an hour, the only one who could make that shot was my brother.

"We can figure that out later," I said not wanting to say what we were both thinking.

"Yeah," he agreed.

"So, if Kuroi isn't tryin' to kill me, how do I stop him from killing me?"

"Gather intel, assess the situation, and come up with a plan," he suggested.

"Right. Who would have intel on Kuroi? Everyone who has known him best is dead."

"Not everyone," Lorenzo suggested telling me what I had to do next.

Keeping eyes on Yuki Sato wasn't something the Ricci pack often did. We knew of her. We had a general idea of how she spent her day. But considering she wasn't Sato's heir apparent, it wasn't a priority.

Having said that, we knew where to find her on any given day if we had to. And now I had to. It being Thursday, she was most likely at the flower market. That made things simple. Because the two of us needed to have a conversation about her brother, and I knew how to find her.

Sitting at a coffee shop across the street from her favorite flower stand, I held up a newspaper and kept an eye out. My intel told me that she bought camellias in the winter and lilies in the summer. It was still lilies season and she would get them in white.

Like clockwork, she appeared. Even without the traditional garb she wore to social events, she was hard to miss. Put together perfectly in a sleeveless summer garden dress, she carried herself with the elegance I once imagined bringing calm to our chaotic Ricci pack. Instead, I ended up with Kuroi. Sure, he was hot as hell. But he was more likely to get us into a war than Matteo was.

Quickly folding my paper and crossing the street, I approached Yuki.

"Yuki, can I talk to you a second."

Instead of being startled, Yuki didn't even look up.

"Mr. Ricci, it is pleasant to see you."

"Pleasant to see you too. Listen, I was wondering if I could talk to you about Kuroi."

That was when she turned around and stared at me.

"It would be improper to involve myself in my brother's marriage."

"Right. Of course. Proper. Yeah, fuck that. I need your help or either me or your brother is gonna end up dead. And, you can rest assured that if something happens to me, everyone in your family is next."

"So, what you're telling me is that I have no choice but to talk to you?" she asked calmly.

"What I'm sayin' is, we gotta talk."

Yuki returned to her shopping.

"Perhaps my honorable brother-in-law would like to join me for tea once my shopping is done."

I didn't like being rescheduled.

"Where?"

"There is a tea shop two blocks from here. Are you familiar with the area?"

I knew where she was referring to. It was where she always went after buying white lilies.

"I know where you're talking about."

"Then I will see you there," she said dismissing me and going about her business.

I had to admit, our interaction didn't go as planned. Everything I personally knew about her made me think that she would bow her head and avert her eyes the whole time. She had more backbone than I would have guessed.

Leaving her to do her thing, I headed to the tea shop and found a table. She did not rush over to join me. It took 45 minutes for her to arrive and by then, I was a little pissed. There was only so long a wolf could sit still.

"Mr. Ricci," she said with a humble bow.

Everything about her was polite. Everything except her actions.

"You're my sister, now. You can call me Dante."

"Very well, Dante."

She stood until I got up and pulled out the seat for her. She then sat quietly staring at me until I had called the server over and had allowed her to order. She was not what I had expected.

"So, your brother, what's his deal?"

"You will have to be more specific," she said never taking her eyes off of me.

"Your father send him to kill me, or what?"

"That is something that you will have to talk to Kuroi or my father about."

"Right," I said not knowing what I was supposed to ask. "Okay, listen. You know your brother."

"I am familiar with him."

"And you know about his reputation."

"I'm not sure which reputation you're referring to."

"I'm talking about the spider demon, one."

Yuki shifted uncomfortably.

"You know, the one where all of his lovers end up dead."

She stared at me without reply.

"Anyway, you know what I'm referring to. But you may also know that whatever shit he's gotten away with in the past, he won't be able to with me."

"If that is the case, then what are you doing here?"

I stared back at her unflinching glare and released my building anger with a chuckle.

"Look, in spite of being, how do I say this? Being surprised by our wedding, I want to make this work. At the very least, I don't want to have to kill him and I don't want to wake up in the middle of the night with a knife in my throat."

"Or not wake up at all," she added.

"Right. So, anything you can tell me about how to handle him or what his deal is, I would be appreciative."

Yuki said nothing else for a while. I knew this negotiation technique. Whoever spoke next lost. That wasn't going to be me. But feeling the pressure, it could have been.

"Are you familiar with the Edo period in Japan, Mr. Ricci?"

I laughed. "No, I might have missed that day in history class. And call me Dante."

"Well, Dante. The Edo period has been popularized by America's fascination with Samurai."

"Oh, okay. Yeah. That's the time with samurai and ninjas and shit. What about it?"

"The Samurai were expected to maintain their honor above all else. And to visit a brothel was considered beneath them. However, what was considered a status symbol was for them to take on a kagema."

"What's a kagema?"

"A kagema was a boy who hadn't yet lost the beauty of youth. It was with them that a samurai would develop a mentor / apprentice relationship."

"Okay," I asked unsure where this was going. "And this has to do with Kuroi how?"

"Our father designated that Kuroi be such a kagema."

I leaned in trying to understand what Yuki was saying.

"Sato made Kuroi one of these, what do you call them?"

"Kagema."

"And what did being a kagema involve?"

It was only then that Yuki's eyes dipped.

"Woah! Your fuckin' father made his own son a prostitute?"

"Isn't that what he is to you? Would I have not been the same if Kuroi didn't have the honor of your hand in marriage?"

I froze. "Different fuckin' thing. Whether I got tricked into it or not, we're married. This ain't any sort of fucked up mentor / apprentice situation."

Yuki took a sip of her tea.

"A rose by a different name."

"Okay, well, that shit don't fly here. If Kuroi doesn't want to be with me, he can grab his stuff and get the fuck out. Nothing's stopping him."

"And yet, he stays," she pointed out.

"Right. He stays." Having heard my words, I considered it.

Why did he stay? Who was I to him? I had heard what Yuki had explained, but this kagema thing couldn't be what I was thinking it was. Not even Sato could do that to his own son. Yuki had to have gotten it wrong. She clearly has some fucked up ideas about marriage.

Though, what would it say about Kuroi if it were true?

No, I won't believe it. Yuki didn't know what she was talking about. I just needed to focus on what I was here for.

"How do I get Kuroi to not kill me?" I asked bluntly.

Yuki took more sips allowing the silence to draw out. I was starting to believe that she was done speaking when she volunteered.

"Kuroi has always responded to a firm hand."

"A firm hand?"

"Kuroi must know his place."

"His place?"

"Mi no hodo wo shiru. Do you know what that means?"

"How the fuck would I know that?"

"It means, to know your place is to know yourself. Kuroi doesn't yet know his place in this world. Perhaps with a strong hand, like yours, he will."

What the fuck did that mean? A strong hand like mine? If she was referring to what I thought she was, that might have been one of the most fucked up things I've ever heard.

If it wasn't for the look in Kuroi's eyes when I had my hands around his neck, I would have dismissed the idea. Had he enjoyed it as I gripped him tighter?

Could she be right? Was that what Kuroi was looking for?

It wouldn't be the craziest idea given that his love taps required stitches. But what exactly did "a firm hand" mean?

To know your place is to know yourself. Leave it to the Japanese to have a phrase for that. At the same time, that was life in a pack. We only functioned as an efficient unit when everyone knew and accepted their role within it.

Had I been so thrown by Kuroi being a man that I had neglected my duty as the head of our new family? Had I failed to lay down the ground rules that would tell him who he was to me and my pack? Had it been because I didn't know?

It hadn't been my choice to marry Kuroi. I had never pictured myself with a husband. But now I had one and he was the hottest fuckin' thing on the planet. So, what Kuroi was to me, was mine. He was mine.

If someone thought they could have him, or even look at him funny, I would take their head off. Touch him and my wolf would go for your throat. He wasn't just under the pack's protection, he was under my protection and would be until the day I died. And if anyone failed to recognize that, including Kuroi, then they would have a rude awakening.

Yuki said nothing else for the rest of our time together. When she was done with her tea, she simply stood, bowed and walked away. I was the one who remained unsure of what to do next.

I knew what I wanted to do. I wanted to run home, grab my hot husband and fuck him raw. We weren't there yet, though. We might never be. But where we were was at the end of my rope. Tonight, something was going to break.

Chapter 7

Kuroi

Well, that didn't work. I had thought that I could be the perfect wife, the perfect Japanese woman. I thought I could be my sister. And all I keep doing is cleaning my husband's blood off the floor.

Oh well. I guess some girls weren't meant for married life. I guess that means I'll die alone. Who would have seen that coming? I would imagine, everybody. I hate it when people are right about me!

So, what went wrong? So many things, but let's start from the beginning. When he arrived home for the first time finding me here, he looked at me funny and I stabbed him. Reasonable.

Next, after slaving in front of the mirror preparing myself, I had dinner waiting for him when he got home, and he laughed at me. In that case, he was just asking to die, wasn't he? If there is a moth and a flame, what can I do about it?

At the same time, I can't help but think that I bear some responsibility for what's happened, somehow. That sounds preposterous considering the effort I've made. Truly, above and beyond. But still, everyone else I've felt something for has died. At some point a girl has to ask, 'Is it me?'

As impossible as it seems, maybe it is. Certainly I've never done anything wrong. If anything extracurricular ever happened with a lover, it was a moth to a flame, just like Dante. Yet, I can't help but think I might have played a role somehow.

No matter, what has passed has passed. Water under the bridge. All I need to worry about now is what I will make for my husband tonight. He never said what he thought about the casserole. Maybe it was too Midwest Americana for him. Dante was Italian. Perhaps I'll prepare spaghetti tonight.

Rummaging through my trunk which remained where it was left in the living room, I found the perfect dress. Very 1950s, Italian countryside. It would require the perfect makeup to pull off. The eyebrows over the white face had to scream portabella.

After spending most of the day designing my outfit, I spent another hour soaking in the master bath's hot tub. All of the day's stress melted away. Refreshed, I moved to the makeup stand I had set up in the guest bath and got to work. When I was finished, I had to wonder where the day had gone. I barely had enough time to order the food before Dante would come home.

Yesterday he had kept me waiting all night. That might have helped to inspire my completely reasonable reaction. No text or call saying, 'Honey, I'm going to be late'? How long had he expected me to stand there? I was wearing heels.

But, that was what wives did, didn't they? Standing waiting dutifully for their husbands? I did my part. I expected him to do his.

Once the food was delivered, I found my husband's spaghetti bowl and dished up. Setting the table, I waited for 6pm to hit, then put on my shoes. To match the countryside style, I chose flat sandals. They weren't flattering for my somewhat masculine feet. But if he didn't like it, he would have to look away.

Taking my position on the edge of the counter within the open floor plan, I would have a clear view of the elevator. When the elevator rang, I would pick up the bowl and the performance would begin.

To my surprise, I didn't have to wait long. Within five minutes of standing there, I heard it. My hubby was home. Grabbing the bowl and presenting it in front of me, I smiled.

There was something different about Dante as he entered this time. His eyes were steel. They scanned the room for me. When I was found, he approached me like a stalking lion. I nearly creamed my panties.

Parked in front of me, he judged what he saw. My makeup was perfect. There wasn't a thread out of place. There was nothing I had gotten wrong.

"No," he proclaimed with authority.

"I'm sorry?" I asked confused by the word.

"I said no."

I didn't know how to respond. I wasn't sure what was going on. Was he trying to tell me what to do?

"Go to the bathroom and wash your face," he ordered.

What? Was he the crazy one? I had spent all day on my face. I was deciding what I would use to hurt him with when he repeated it.

"I said, go to the bathroom and wash your face," this time saying it with an emphasis on every word.

"No," I replied unsure what either of us would do next.

Dante tilted his head surprised. He was clearly a man who was used to getting what he wanted. But he was going to have to learn that I wasn't one of his yes men. More than that, he was ruining our moment.

Ignoring all of that, he slowly paced in front of me, his eyes never leaving me. If I didn't know better, I would think he was deciding whether or not to shift and eat me.

"I have let you get away with some crazy shit since you've been here…"

"You have let me…?"

"I am speaking!" he demanded.

I paused, having been spoken to like this before but in an entirely different context. When it was clear that I wouldn't interrupt him again, he continued.

"I have let you get away with some crazy shit since you've been here, but no more. From now on, you will do what I tell you to do, and nothing more. Do you understand me?"

I was… confused. Listening to him speak, a wave of heat washed through me. It was a rush.

"And, if I don't?" I challenged.

He stared at me unflinchingly.

"Then you will be punished."

My breath hitched. My heart raced.

"I would like to see you try."

Dante stepped back caging his rage. Fear and arousal battled within me. Stiffening his spine, he stepped inches in front of me and the spaghetti bowl. I could feel his heat. I could practically smell his wolf. It was intoxicating.

"Kuroi," he began in a low rumbling voice, "go to the bathroom and wash your face."

I trembled barely able to contain myself. I had to open my mouth to breathe. Gripping the bowl preparing to defend myself, I drew air into my lungs and whispered, "No."

He didn't respond but anger pulsed off of him. When he moved, I realized that I hadn't prepared for his blow. Flinching for the impact, it never came. Instead, he headed to the kitchen turning his back on me.

Watching him, he retrieved a wooden spoon from the utensils drawer and turned out the chair at the head of the dining room table. Sitting, he looked at me. I swear I could see his wolf staring at me through his eyes.

"Come here."

I opened my mouth to protest. He cut me off. "Now!"

What could I do? I heard him. I was to come to him. So, placing the bowl on the counter, I went to him. Standing at his feet, I trembled like a schoolboy.

"Kneel. Across my knee."

Oh my god. My heart thumped. My head spun. I fought to resist but couldn't. Lowering to my knees, I bent over with my stomach on his legs.

When the first strike hit, my skin was electric. My body tingled. After the wave of shock had barreled through me, a sting spread across my ass that took my breath away.

The second was more intense. The third made me moan.

"Ahh," I groaned knowing he hadn't held back. His power had made me weak in the knees. So when he next told me to get up, I wasn't sure I could.

Swallowing as the heat billowed around my neck, I flinched as the sting of his strikes spread. Fighting through it to my feet, all I could do was look down at him. His anger was gone, but I could still see his wolf.

"Now, go to the bathroom and wash your face. When you're done, we will sit and enjoy the meal you have prepared."

Without a word, I did what he had commanded. I didn't want to wash off the hours of work I had done, but I was compelled to do what he said. It was like he had a power over me.

I had heard that alpha wolves had a voice that their pack couldn't disobey? Was that why I was doing what he told me to do? Because he was my alpha? But I wasn't a wolf. Could he still have made me a part of his pack?

Staring into my makeup mirror, I took a breath and grabbed a towel. Stripping away the layers slowly, what was revealed underneath was burnt and ugly. I looked away. I had done what he had commanded. All that was left was to return to him.

Remembering the force in his voice, I took another breath and did what I was told. Exiting the bathroom, I entered the living room. Unable to look up, I approached the dining table finding him seated. Retrieving the spaghetti bowl, I placed it on the table and took a seat next to him.

Still unable to meet his eyes, I sat listening to him dish up. When he was done, I knew it was my turn but I couldn't move. I couldn't look up at him. I couldn't get up. All I could do was sit there meekly. This wasn't me. Yet, here I was.

"Kuroi," Dante said drawing my attention.

I turned to him without meeting his gaze.

"Look at me," he said softly. When I didn't, he repeated it with authority. "Look at me!"

I did. His eyes were different. The wolf was gone. What was left was softer, kind.

"I don't want you to think that I don't like your makeup and dresses. Believe me, I do. You look beautiful."

"I don't," I admitted no longer able to hold his gaze.

Leaning across the table he took my chin between his fingers. His touch sent shivers of pleasure through me. Lifting my chin, I settled in his eyes.

"I said, believe me. You do."

"Then, why?"

Dante let go of my chin and this time was the one to look away. Scanning his plate, it was a moment before he returned to me vulnerably.

"Because we have been married for three days and I barely know what my husband looks like. I would like to meet him."

"You will be disappointed," I admitted.

"Let me be the judge. Will you do that?"

I didn't respond. He took it as agreement.

"Good. And so you know, so far, I like what I see," he said with a smile.

He smiled. My husband smiled at me. Why? What did it mean? All I knew was that I liked it. I shouldn't have, considering he was clearly a bad judge of character. But he was… sweet.

"Now," Dante said relaxing, "will you join me for this excellent meal you prepared?"

I was thinking about telling him that I had bought it, but why ruin the moment. Dishing a little of it onto my plate, I dug in realizing I hadn't thought things all the way through. I hated spaghetti. Always had. So sitting there eating it, I considered if being forced to eat something I didn't like was my fault too.

Our meal continued in silence and ended as quietly. Clearing the table like a domestic goddess, I returned to my seat knowing our first true conversation wasn't done.

"Your stuff is still in the living room," he eventually said staring at my trunks.

"I didn't know where to put it," I admitted feeling the pinch of shame.

"I see," he replied thinking for a moment. "You can move yourself into the spare room. You can get comfortable and consider it yours."

"No," I said without a second of thought.

"No?"

"No," I repeated as a matter of fact.

"Why not?"

"Because I am your husband. As your husband, I will share your bed."

"No!" he replied sharply. It was harsh enough for me to think it would lead to another fight. But instead, his eyes dipped. "Look, you have to understand that this is all new to me. I didn't plan to be married to you."

"You thought it would be Yuki," I said stating the obvious.

His head bobbled without answering.

"It doesn't matter what I thought. I just didn't expect this. I'm not saying it isn't good or that I won't get used to it. I just need a moment."

"I understand. You can have your moment." I paused. "Moment over."

Dante looked at me and laughed.

"You have your rules. I have mine. If I am going to be married, which like you, I had no choice in, I will share my husband's bed."

"You didn't want to do this?" Dante said melting a little.

"Did I want to marry a complete stranger and bear his children?"

"There might be something Sato didn't tell you about the birds and the bees," he joked.

"The answer is no, I didn't want this. I was tricked into it just like you."

Dante looked at me with disappointment. It surprised me.

"So, what do we do about it?" he asked.

I allowed the question to hang in the air.

"We compromise," I suggested.

Dante looked at me intrigued.

"How's that?"

"We do our duties to our family and our marriage," I said with a hint of a smile.

"And where's the compromise?" he asked amused.

"You don't see it?" I joked.

Dante laughed. It was a good laugh. It filled me with warmth.

"I don't."

"Fine. The compromise is that, while you get used to this, I will only spend a few nights a week in your bed."

"One night."

"Seven," I countered.

Dante laughed again.

"Three."

"Four," I compromised.

He stared at me with an impish smile. It felt good.

"Alright, four. But, my rule stands true. You must do what I tell you to do when I tell you."

I was offended. "Or what?"

"Or, you will be punished again."

His suggestion sent a rush through me that made me lightheaded.

"Are you threatening me with a good time?"

"I'm serious."

"So am I," I confirmed.

We both stared at each other. I was starting to see something emerge in him. It aroused me. Was he going to be punishing me on a regular basis?

"If you don't follow my rules, I will punish you," he confirmed suggestively.

"And what happens if I do follow your rules?"

"I'll punish you more," he replied with a devilish smile.

My cock became rock hard. With the lingering sting of his paddling fading, I wanted more. To my great surprise, I restrained myself. Who knew I was capable? But even I could see that we were in a delicate negotiation. And there was still one thing left to discuss.

"So, where should I put my things?"

Dante thought about that.

"And, if I said the spare room?"

"I would again say no," I said with a smile.

"Alright. You can put it in my bedroom."

"Our bedroom," I corrected.

"We'll see."

"We'll see. And did I tell you that our sleeping together starts tonight?"

I couldn't tell if it was panic or pleasure that took over Dante.

"You're just sayin' the same bed, right? That's all?" he confirmed.

"We'll see," I said with a smile.

"Kuroi!"

"Fine. I hope I don't do anything that makes you punish me," I teased.

"I've made a mistake, haven't I?" he joked.

"Not from where I'm sitting," I said truly seeing my husband for the first time.

He was not the man I thought he was. I was expecting a brute. It was what I expected from all men. He was different. I couldn't put my finger on how, but he was.

"Why don't you get ready for bed. I'll be in there in a second," I told him.

"Take your time. I need to take a shower."

I nodded. "Let me know if you need any help in there," I said with a smile.

He looked at me accusingly.

"Getting undressed," I explained.

His suspicion deepened.

"Because of your injuries!"

"Right, my injuries," my wolf shifter husband said doubtfully.

He wasn't wrong.

Waiting a respectful amount of time, I eventually headed to his bedroom. Entering, I found the bathroom door open. Approaching and leaning on the door frame, I found him shirtless in a pair of sweatpants. Once I saw the bulge in them, it was all that I could look at. My pulse raced imagining his bulge pushing into me.

"You sleeping in that?" he asked snapping me back.

I looked down at my dress. A part of me felt foolish for wearing it. It was like I was walking around offstage with my costume on.

"No. Can you help me with the zipper?"

"Yeah," he said approaching me slowly.

When I felt the heat from his shower envelop me, I breathed him in and turned my back to him. Waiting for his touch, when it came, it sent shivers through my body.

With the back of his fingers touching my neck as he gripped the top of my dress, he slowly unzipped me. When he was done, the back of his hand brushed my ass. Was it intentional?

Feeling heat in my cheeks, I turned around with barely any space between us. He didn't budge. Neither did I. Lowering the sleeves over my shoulders, I let the dress drop.

Still inches from him, I looked up into his eyes and subtly showed him my neck. I wanted him to want it. He didn't move. So, when I stepped out of my dress wearing only my lacy pink panties, he got a good look.

"Are you ready for bed?" I asked turning so he could see my round ass.

"You make me unsure of everything," he replied.

"You don't have to be unsure about me," I told him before getting into bed and settling on a pillow looking up into his eyes.

Having finished my show, I watched him as he stepped out of the bathroom. He made no grand gesture. He didn't have to. His increased bulge said it all and seeing it made me tingle.

Sitting on his side of the bed, he reached for the light and then got in. For a moment, it was dark. I felt him next to me. Staring at the ceiling, I wondered what I should do next. I wanted to test him. I wanted to feel his bulging cock.

But, wasn't this his test for me? He had asked that nothing happen between us. At least, not tonight. I could do that. I mean, I could kind of do that.

But everything in me screamed to roll over, slip his thick cock into my mouth, and push it down my throat. I wasn't going to. Not tonight. It would kill me having him so close, but I would prove that he could trust me.

Obviously he could only trust me so far, because I couldn't do nothing with him next to me. Smelling his slight musk over the sheets and pillow, I was as hard as I could be. I needed to at least touch him. So, making a show of it to let him know I was coming, I rolled onto my side, slipped my arm around him onto his chest, and spooned him.

My hard cock found his ass cheeks. It sat in the crevice perfectly. For tonight, it would have to be enough. Pressing my chest against his back, I rested my cheek on his shoulder. It felt so good that I rotated it. It was all I could do to keep myself from fully breaking his trust.

That didn't last, but not because I gave up. After a few short minutes, Dante shook me off of him while trying to roll over. I moved away disappointed until he kept rolling making himself my big spoon.

His large hands spread across my chest. His hard bulge pressed against my ass. And his warm breath flowed across my neck relaxing me more than ever in my life.

Was this what feeling safe felt like? Thinking about it, I slowly fell asleep.

Chapter 8

Dante

Waking up with my arms wrapped around the most beautiful man I've ever seen, all I could think was, 'What the hell am I doing?' This wasn't me. Yeah, I'd been with a few guys. But I didn't wake up with them in my arms.

For the most part, everyone knew the drill when they came over. It was a quick fix and out the door. There were no feelings involved. We were both just satisfying an urge. They were there to get enough of what we both needed to tide us over until the next time.

Yet here I was holding onto Kuroi not wanting to let go. I had to let go, though. I couldn't lose myself in whatever was going on here. I had a job that needed my focus. Take my eye off things for a moment and that's when you end up dead.

Still, the man I was with this time was my husband. Until death do us part. This was it. He wasn't going anywhere. I had to come up with a new life that included him.

Would that new life regularly include bending him over my knee for a spoon across his ass? God, I hoped so. I had never been more turned on in my life. I don't know why. I can't explain it. But hearing him react to every stroke, made me feel like what was going on was real.

In a world where everybody lies telling you what they think you want to hear, there's nothing you can believe. But pain is real. The body has its limits. Pass a threshold and no one can fake it.

With his getups and crazy comments, I can't tell what's real with Kuroi. But when I let loose on his ass and he squealed, I knew that I had found him. Having him, I could have stripped him down and fucked him right there.

That was probably why I agreed to let him move into my room. I would have agreed to anything with him looking at me like that. I can't let myself get weak like that in front of him, though.

His goddamn body was a drug. I keep needing more. Even now it's taking everything I have not to push my throbbing cock against his ass asking it to let me in.

The feel of his lean body in my arms. The hint of citrus in his hair. He was a walking aphrodisiac. I had to keep him at a safe distance. Lose focus for a second and who will I become?

I was willing to lay there all morning wanting something from him I couldn't have. Then he squirmed and backed into me. Already holding him, only one thing had changed. His firm ass was now pressed against my hard cock.

I froze wanting it and knowing I couldn't have it. So when he wiggled his ass inviting me in, I let him go and sprung out of bed.

"Where are you going?" he asked in a raspy morning voice.

"Gotta get ready for work," I said, headed to the bathroom without looking back.

"I wanna come," he said sweetly.

I stopped and looked at him. This was the first time he had asked me for something so nicely before. Shit, how was I supposed to refuse, especially with his large beautiful eyes staring at me like that?

"I don't think that would be a good idea," I said with no fight in me.

"Is it because you're ashamed of being married to me? You think I'd embarrass you?"

I got defensive.

"I'm not ashamed of you. I don't care what anyone says about it. You're my husband and anyone who has a problem with it will have my fist down their throat."

"Then, why can't I come?"

"It's just that…"

"Is it the dresses? I know how to be professional."

"It's not about the dresses."

It was a little about the dresses. Don't get me wrong, I fuckin' loved them. And I didn't know that it was something I could be into until I saw him in his wedding gown.

But I wasn't sure how well his dresses and elaborate makeup would go over with the family considering, if Matteo had tried to kill me, it would have been at our father's order. And if Pa did order it, it would have been for allowing Sato to humiliate the family by marrying me to his son.

"Then, why can't I come?"

"I didn't say you couldn't. I just don't think it's a good idea right now," I told him before retreating into the bathroom and closing the door. "Besides, don't you have to spend today unpacking your stuff," I yelled as I stared at the liar in the mirror.

"I don't have that much stuff."

"Still, maybe it's not a good idea yet."

And that was where we both left it. Getting dressed and powering past him as he watched me from the bed, he didn't ask again. And when I yelled back that I was headed to work and that I would see him tonight, we had resolved our first disagreement. Maybe being married to him wasn't going to be as hard as I thought.

Getting into work earlier than usual, I took a moment to appreciate the quiet. This whole thing really was a mess. And I wasn't just talking about the killer I was sharing my bed with. There was someone else who was trying to kill me. That someone could be my brother.

When my assistant popped in to give me my mail, I refocused on what I had to do today. One of the changes I had made from how my father ran things was to treat the business more professionally. We were long past the times when keeping two sets of accounting was enough. Now we laundered money by investing in real estate and crypto. The reports generated from our investments were never ending.

Everything needed my approval and my sign off. Beyond that, I needed to make sure the business benefitted from my new connection with the Yakuza. If I wanted father to accept my marriage and not try to off me, he needed to see the upside of me being with Kuroi.

"Got a second?" Lorenzo asked leaning into my office.

"What's up?" I replied inviting him in.

Closing the door behind him, Lorenzo entered and sat in the chair on the other side of my desk smiling.

"You gonna sit there grinning like an idiot or do you have something to say to me?"

"Any new stitches last night?"

I stared at my brother wondering where this was coming from. He had been the one to stitch me up the last time I needed it. So, it was a legitimate question. But that look on his face… And how many questions would follow?

Falling asleep with Kuroi in my arms had been one of the best feelings of my life. God damn if holdin' him didn't do things to me. But did Lorenzo need to see that part of my life? I was his big brother and the alpha of his pack. I wasn't ready for him to view me any differently.

No, for now, my life with Kuroi would be between the two of us. No one else needed to know or see anything. All they needed to know was that the Ricci pack and the Yakuza in New York were of one mind. There was no getting between us.

"No fuckin' stitches. Let's leave it at that."

"Got it," Lorenzo said becoming more serious. "There's one other thing we haven't talked about."

"Yeah? What's that?"

"Who tried to kill you."

He was right. We hadn't since realizing that Matteo was the only one capable of shooting me in the neck while I drove.

Lorenzo continued, "Am I gonna be the one to say it or are you?"

"What's that?"

"Pa could have hired a hit out on you."

"We don't know that."

"We don't know anything. But we do know who could have shot you in the neck if that is what happened. And we know you've given him reason to order the hit."

"Listen Lorenzo, I know you have your problems with Pa. But ordering a hit out on me? Come on."

"What about Uncle Vinny?"

Uncle Vinny was like the boogie man in our household growing up. Legend had it that he crossed my father thinking he could become alpha. He should have challenged Pa to a fight. If he had, everything would have been fine, even if he had lost. Pa probably would have gotten him pretty good, but Uncle Vinny would have been allowed to stay in the pack.

But supposedly, Uncle Vinny teamed with a vampire coven to take Pa out. When Pa discovered this, he sent the pack to slaughter the blood suckers and slit Uncle Vinny's throat. They got all of the vampires, but couldn't find my uncle.

The story goes that when he turned up again, he was back in Italy. He was under the protection of a new pack and the only time we heard from him was at Christmas. He would call asking to speak to Pa and Pa would refuse.

"None of us knows what actually happened between the two of them. It could have been anything," I told Lorenzo.

My brother looked at me confused.

"Why are you suddenly defending him?"

"I'm not defending him. You accused him of putting a hit out on his own son and I'm tryin' to look at things logically."

"You're fuckin' defendin' him. After the hell he put us through growing up."

"He raised us to survive. You don't prepare a wolf for a life on the beach."

"What the fuck, Dante?"

Yeah, I heard it. Lorenzo was right. I was making excuses for the shit way he treated us growing up. I could understand why Matteo would do it. But after everything that happened, why would I?

"I'm just sayin' that the way he raised us turned us into the men we are today."

"Yeah. Men who can't be sure if our brother tried to kill you."

I was about to make another excuse for our father. I could feel it coming until the intercom on my phone buzzed.

"There's someone coming in. I couldn't stop him," Silvie said sending me reaching for my gun.

Before I got hold of the one fastened to the underside of my desk, my office door flung open. The panic in Silvie's voice had told me everything I thought I needed to know. My heart stopped waiting for a bullet.

But with my finger gripping the trigger and a 50/50 chance of shooting them through the backside of my desk, a familiar face appeared. Standing in the doorway, he stared at me and squinted.

"Is that a gun in your hand? Or are you just happy to see me?"

"Kuroi? What are you doing here?" I asked panicked in a new way.

"Can't a boy come to see where his new husband works?" he asked entering and closing the door behind him.

"I thought we agreed…"

"We agreed to nothing. I said I wanted to see where you worked and here I am. And, Honey, it's probably a good idea for you to take your hand off that gun before I take offense."

Kuroi was being flamboyant and playful, but I didn't let it fool me. I knew what he was capable of so I let go of my gun.

"Good," he said before turning to a surprised Lorenzo. "You were at our wedding, weren't you? You're one of the brothers?" Kuroi looked at me. "I have so many now. It's hard to keep track."

"Yeah. I was at the wedding. Lorenzo," he said offering him his hand with an all too friendly smile.

Seeing Lorenzo's smile and the way Kuroi looked back at him, made my wolf want to jump across the desk and rip my brother's throat out.

"Kuroi. Charmed," he said flirting with my brother.

"Seriously, Kuroi, what are you doing here?" I said demanding my flirtatious husband's attention back on me before someone got hurt.

"I told you…" he said playfully.

"And I told you."

"Yet, here we are," he said before taking the far seat next to the window. "Please, don't let me interrupt. I just want to see my man in action."

He had to know this was pissing me off, right? He had intentionally disobeyed my order. He had to know that I would punish him for this. Or, maybe that was the point.

My growing cock flinched thinking about what I would do to him when we got home. One, he had come here without my permission. And he had done it unannounced. That was two. Unfortunately he wasn't wearing a dress or makeup that I could see, so I couldn't punish him for that.

The suit he wore appeared to be a woman's suit, but damn did he look good in it. Grey pinstriped, buttonless jacket attached at the breast, with the sleeves rolled up. And a collarless white blouse with the chest cut out. If my brother wasn't here, I would fuck him just for coming here looking like that.

"I, ahh, should go," Lorenzo volunteered.

"No, please, stay. Pretend I'm not here."

Lorenzo looked at me for what to do. I wasn't sure. He was my husband but he was also Sato's son. At the same time, I didn't get the sense that Sato gave him much of a reason for loyalty. Still, fathers have a way of getting into your head.

"Let's just pretend he's not there. I'm sure he'll sit there quietly," I said looking at him.

"Like a mouse," Kuroi said pleased.

Lorenzo looked at me questioning if I was sure.

"Anyway, as I was saying. We can't jump to any conclusions about who is trying to kill me," I said for Kuroi's benefit.

"Someone's trying to kill you?" Kuroi said suddenly sitting up. "Who?"

Lorenzo looked at me and laughed.

"We're trying to eliminate the suspects," I explained.

"Who's on the list?"

Lorenzo jumped in. "Well, the first person on the list is you."

"Doesn't make sense. If I wanted to kill him, he would be dead by now. Who else?"

Lorenzo looked at me questioningly. I took over.

"Sato is another."

"Possible. But the most likely person he would send to do it would be me and again, you're not already dead. Next."

"How do we know you're not playing the long game?" Lorenzo questioned.

"Dante, Honey," he said playfully, "have you not told him how impatient I am?"

"No, Honey, I haven't mentioned anything about you because I keep my business and private life separate," I said through clenched teeth.

"Oh, that's how you treat hookups. I'm your husband 'til death do us part," he said with a smile that would've made me pee my pants if I still thought he was sent to kill me. "So, who else?" he asked impatiently.

I looked at Lorenzo for a last minute reason for why I shouldn't tell him. My brother didn't provide it.

"One person who might have a reason to get rid of me is…" I took a breath before admitting it, "our father."

Kuroi thought about it. "I could see that."

"You can? Why?" I asked surprised.

"You're younger, you're stronger, you're smarter. You're a threat."

"A threat to what? I'm running the family business. His pack."

"Exactly. His pack and you're running it. That could make a person feel a certain way."

"A way to make a wolf put a hit out on his son instead of fighting him for it?" I asked both offended and shocked.

"You're younger, stronger, and smarter. If I were him and wanted my pack back, ordering a hit would be how I would do it," Kuroi volunteered.

"You would have your son killed for taking over the family business?"

"That would depend."

"On what?"

"Did I give it to him or did he take it. If he took it and I wasn't ready to let go," Kuroi gestured across his neck.

Lorenzo replied, "But in your case, it would be more like," and clutched his heart pretending to have a heart attack.

Kuroi looked at Lorenzo with fire in his eyes. I braced myself. Looks couldn't kill but Kuroi could.

"I think what my brother is saying is that your reputation precedes you."

"Oh, thank you!" Kuroi responded taking it as a compliment. He turned to Lorenzo. "And I'm sure if anyone gave a fuck about who you were, your reputation would precede you, too."

Lorenzo squirmed taking the insult on the chin.

"Anyway," I interrupted. "You aren't our father. So, I don't know how relevant your opinion is."

Kuroi leaned forward engaged.

"Tell me this, if your father were to send someone after you, who would it be?"

I looked at Lorenzo again.

"If he sent someone, the most-likely person would be Matteo."

"The psycho who killed one of my father's men and then tied him to the back of a car to drag through Yakuza territory?"

"Yes. Our brother, Matteo."

"Oh, he would totally kill you."

Lorenzo laughed. I wasn't sure why.

"You don't know that," I said dismissively.

"I'm saying he's capable of killing you. I didn't say he's tried."

Lorenzo's eyes jumped between the two of us. "So, we're just gonna ignore that all of his lovers died from a heart attack, and you could've had one before the crash?"

"A heart attack caused your crash?" Kuroi asked surprised.

"I did not have a heart attack! Or a panic attack. Or anything else!"

"Then why did you run into a tree?" Kuroi asked, concern shaping his tone.

"I felt a pinch in my neck moments before I blacked out. The working theory is that someone shot me."

"Let me guess," Kuroi replied, "the only person you know who could make that shot is your brother, Matteo?"

I looked at Lorenzo for a way out of this. I didn't get one.

"Yeah."

"I can find out for you," Kuroi said casually.

"What?"

"Get me in the same room with him. I can find out if he was the one who tried to kill you."

"You are not torturing my brother!" I said feeling my wolf's protective rage.

"Geez, calm down. I didn't say anything about torturing him. I just need to talk to him. Where can we do it?" he asked enthusiastically.

Kuroi was serious and excited. What made him think he could find out something like that? Sure, Matteo wasn't the most sophisticated person I knew, but my brother knew how to keep his mouth shut.

When I didn't reply, Kuroi added, "Come on, put me in the same room as him. I'll find out for you."

When Lorenzo and I remained silent he mentioned, "You're my husband. We're going to end up in the same room together eventually. So, sooner or later, it is going to happen. And if it happens after he's killed you, I would have to kill him."

"Come on, Dante, you would be saving two lives here," Lorenzo joked.

I leaned back in my office chair and thought. Kuroi wasn't wrong. They were gonna end up in the same room eventually. And something told me Kuroi wasn't going to let this go. Maybe it was better if I had control over how and where it happened.

"Matteo had suggested the three of us having dinner together."

"Wait, I thought we were supposed to have dinner together first," Lorenzo reminded me.

"Ah, that's so sweet," Kuroi cooed. "And if you're ever suspected of killing my husband, believe me, I would be the first person you would see," he said in a more threatening baby voice than I thought possible.

"Luckily, we don't have to worry about that, because Lorenzo is the most loyal brother I have."

"Let's hope so. So, when do I get to meet the traitor?"

"We don't know he's a traitor. We don't even know if our father is making a move against me."

"Then it's time to find out. Set up the dinner and let me know when. I'll prepare a meal fit for my king," he said getting up and heading to the door.

"Actually, I'll set it up at Maramar. They have a cannoli you have to try."

Kuroi, who had his hand on the knob, looked back at me. It was obvious that I was choosing a public setting to limit the extracurricular activities by either of them. I half expected Kuroi to insist, but he didn't. I guess that only meant I had three things to punish him for, the third being speaking when he said he wouldn't.

"Arrange it for tonight," Kuroi said relenting.

"It will be for tomorrow night. We have plans tonight," I told him showing my displeasure with my eyes.

Looking back at me, he nearly whimpered. "Oh right, our plans. I'll be dressed and ready when you get home."

His words made my dick hard. Watching him go, I imagined his small waist gripped between my large hands and the feeling of the front of my thighs against the back of his. I would make him moan.

"You two have plans tonight?" Lorenzo asked me when he was gone. "Have you two been seen out together yet?"

"It's not that type of plan," I said revealing more than I should have but too aroused to stop myself.

After debating the wisdom of allowing Kuroi to have dinner with Matteo first, I said the final word on it and the dinner was arranged. With a lot of things left to do for the day, there was only one thing I could think of—how I was going to punish Kuroi for disobeying me.

There were a lot of things I could do. But which should I employ. In the end, I had to do some research. He was clearly more familiar with being punished than I was with punishing. But one thing I was good at was pushing a body to its physical limits to get what I want. I wanted Kuroi, so I would have to push him.

I was never one for shopping, but the shopping trip that followed, I liked. It was at a shop in the heart of

Harlem. The place had a lot of options. Imagining how I could use each on Kuroi made my cock throb.

After spending an hour browsing, I left the shop with a few things. I could barely stop myself from running every light on the way home. When I parked, I had to take a breath to get my dick to calm down. Collecting my bags and entering the elevator, I felt my wolf take over me.

Entering my apartment, the living room was empty.

"Kuroi, come here now!" I said, my wolf awash in fury and lust.

Kuroi exited my bedroom meekly. He had been in my room. Yet another thing to punish him for. Wearing a Japanese robe embroidered with gold silk, he approached me, lowered his head and said, "Yes, Sir?"

Hearing it, my cock again flashed hard. With him in front of me, I imagined pushing my fingers across his mahogany skin.

"You showed up at my office without my permission."

"Yes Sir," he replied with his head still lowered.

"What did I say I would do if you didn't follow my rules?"

"You said you would punish me, Sir."

"That's right. And yet you did it anyway. Did you want to be punished?"

"Yes, Sir."

"Are you ready for your punishment?"

"Yes, Sir."

"On your knees."

Without lifting his head, Kuroi got onto his knees.

"Now stay."

"Is this my punishment?"

"You will speak when spoken to. Is that clear?"

"Yes, Sir."

Leaving him on his knees with his head bowed, I retreated to my room to prepare. Setting everything in place, I savored the moment. Taking a hot shower, I felt every drop as the steaming water touched my skin. I felt alive.

Putting on a silk robe, I reentered the living room to find that Kuroi hadn't moved. Watching his motionless body, I grabbed a drink and slowly drank it waiting for another reason to punish him. He didn't give me one.

So, instead, I returned to a spot in front of him and told him to get up. He did without looking at me.

"Go to my room," I ordered sternly.

He did and I followed. When he had entered and stopped, I passed him, stood next to the dresser and presented what was on top of it.

"For disobeying me, you will choose," I said pointing at the crop and flog which contrasted with the white cloth beneath them. "Each will come with a unique series of disciplines. Do you understand?"

"Yes, Sir."

"You will take it. If you can no longer take it, you will say the word cherries. Nothing else will get me to stop. Do you understand?"

"Yes, Sir."

"Say it."

"No, Sir."

"Why not?" I asked my temper flaring.

"Because I don't want you to stop."

I calmed and smiled.

"Choose."

"Can I have both, Sir?"

"Your punishment is that you must choose."

I saw that he was getting it. If he were good, he might have gotten both. But because he had disobeyed me, he could only have one never knowing what he had passed up.

"Please, Sir, may I have both."

"I said choose! ...Or you will get none."

It was only then that he looked at me, lust and fear shining in his eyes. Hurrying to the dresser he looked down at them.

"May I touch them, Sir?"

"No," I said furthering his punishment. "Choose."

Hovering his hands over the two, he shook with desire.

"I said choose!"

"The flog," he spat pining over what he had chosen.

"Very well," I said removing the crop and placing it in the drawer.

His desire had weakened him. Seeing it made my cock pulse. My wolf wanted him so badly that it tore at my insides fighting to get out. But I was the one who had to teach Kuroi a lesson.

"Strip," I told him, my heart pounding at the thought of him.

Without hesitation, Kuroi turned to me and slowly lowered his robe. He was naked underneath. His lean lines were highlighted by taut muscles. He was more beautiful than any statue. My skin tingled at the sight of him.

More than that, his generous cock was hard. Shaved to almost nothing, it stood out. I wanted to feel it in my hands. I wanted to caress his small balls. The thought of it overwhelmed me.

Gathering myself and my wolf, I pulled two handcuffs out of another drawer. Placing them on the dresser next to the flog, I addressed him.

"Cuff one to either hand."

He did without hesitation. With both secured, he looked up at me with desire.

"Now, follow me," I told him grabbing the flog and crossing into the living room to the balcony's sliding glass door.

With him waiting, I lowered the lights behind us. With the city lights brightening in front of us, I led him to the railing and told him to grip it. Obeying, he parted his lips struggling for breath.

I imagined what he felt as the cool night air caressed his sweat-kissed skin. And pressing my robe-covered hard cock against him as I leaned around him, I said, "Now anyone watching will see what happens when you disobey me," I told him as I handcuffed him to the railing.

"Yes, Sir. Please teach me how to obey."

"I will teach you how to obey," I whispered in his ear as he whimpered from the heat.

Leaving him shivering, I stepped back and lit him up. When the leather strands touched his ass, his head whipped back. I hadn't shown him mercy.

"Thank you, Sir," he purred.

Hearing that, I stroked him again. His body shivered as his bare ass slowly striped red. Brushing his marked spots with the leather, I waited for him to relax before striping him again. When his body contracted, my cock flinched.

"More, Sir," he begged.

I swiped him again and again, turned on more each time. When I lowered my aim to the back of his legs, he groaned. He hadn't been ready for it. And when his legs started dancing, I lost control. Striking him harder and harder, I finally grabbed his curled chest, nipped his ear, and found his hole with the tip of my cock.

"Yes?" I moaned.

"Yes," he begged.

And without hesitation, I allowed my dripping juices to paint a path past his tight opening into his depths.

"Ahhh," he groaned feeling my girth pry him open.

His warmth consumed my cock. The pleasure rippled through me. Biting his ear to contain myself, I pushed until I couldn't go deeper. Gripping his hip, I trust harder until he bellowed in painful ecstasy.

Buried within him, I slid my hand up his naked chest to his throat. Its width disappeared into my grasp. Squeezing, I felt his helpless to my will. I could do whatever I wanted to him. And feeling the night's cool breeze circle between our tingling skin, I pulled back enough to strum his insides.

"Yes. Yes!" he crooned, with my hand around his throat and my groin thumping his ass.

My mind swam loving every moment with him. His body in my arms, his ass around my cock, the way he squealed and moaned with my thrusts.

Fucking him harder and harder, his legs began to give way. The longer I rode him, the more I held him erect. He was melting in my arms. And when I slipped him hand under his stomach and lifted his feet off the ground, I knew what was next.

Still holding him and with my cock in his ass, I leaned past him and yanked the handcuffs off the railing. Free, I pulled his back to my chest and walked to my bedroom. I was still inside of him. He felt a part of me. Hooking his feet around my legs and his hand around my head, he had attached himself to me. So, when I lowered him onto the bed, I had to detach myself from his grip to get what I wanted next.

Perching him on his knees with his ass in the air, I pressed his chest to the bed and moved above him. Memorized by him, I fucked him without mercy. The bed shock as my groin hit his flesh. I felt like I was trying to fuck my way into him. I wanted to wear him or make him a part of me. I didn't know which. But when I couldn't take being so far from him any longer, I flipped him over, pressed his knees to his chest and fucked him while finding his lips.

I didn't kiss guys. I fucked them. Why would I ever want to be that close? But with Kuroi, I didn't know who I was. Being with him did something to me. And when our lips touched and his parted, I let go.

As incredible as his ass was, it was our kiss that made me cum. His mouth was small. So was his tongue.

But twisting together, they were perfect for each other. Its sensation robbed me of my will.

We continued to kiss even as I groaned. I was filling him with my juices. That was when I remembered Kuroi's pleasure. Reaching between us for is cock, my touch made it jump.

Pushing my finger down his shaft, I found that he had already cum. He had been as turned on as I was. He had cum without either of us touching him. Had the way I reshaped his hole been for him what our kiss had been for me?

I didn't know and quickly, I didn't care. All I could think about was returning to his mouth. Kuroi had been my first kiss. Sure, I had kissed women. But they had never mattered to me. I was just doing what a man was supposed to do. I didn't even know how it was supposed to feel until Kuroi parted his lips and let me inside.

Now that I had kissed him, I never wanted to stop. Kuroi was mine. No one would ever again touch him.

Pulling my shrinking cock out of him, I pushed my fingers into his curly hair and cradled him as I rolled him on top of me. I never stopped kissing him. I couldn't.

Feeling Kuroi's cum press between us, I flexed my ass sliding him against me. It didn't take long for me to get hard again. Surprised, Kuroi reached down and took hold of my cock. Pulling away from my lips long enough to laugh, he returned before slowly moving down to my chin, then neck, chest, and stomach.

With his delicate fingers still holding me, I pulsed feeling his lips get closer. He wasn't ready for that yet, though. And finding the ridges of my stomach muscles, he rubbed his sharp cheekbones against them tracing the trenches with the tip of his nose.

Eventually when there wasn't another inch to explore, he continued his path down, pressed my large cock to the side of his face, and traced the rim of its head with the tip of his tongue. When he got his fill, he plunged my mushroom onto the back his throat.

I didn't expect much when it came to this. Others had tried to swallow me, but I was too big. Kuroi also tried. He pushed onto it until he choked. Backing off, he tried again until his body contracted and tears rolled down his cheeks.

"I'm big," I pointed out giving him permission to give up. He didn't.

Focusing more on stroking me as he sucked, he teased my head until my toes danced. Kuroi knew what he was doing. When I felt like I would explode, he backed off walking the edge. He tortured me like this for longer than I thought possible.

"Please," I begged him needing badly to cum.

It was only then that he looked up at me with a Cheshire cat smile. He knew what he had been doing, that fucker. And finally ready to release me, he clutched my balls with his small hand and squeezed.

When I came, I was a volcano. I couldn't stop cumming. When all of the fluid in me had erupted, I didn't stop.

My entire body was as sensitive as fuck. Brushing his hand and mouth off of me, the bastard laughed as he returned his hands making my cock jump. It was like being hit by a bolt of lightning.

"You're a fuckin' sadist," I told him, shaking my head in amusement.

"What? Don't you like me touching your cock?"

He touched it again making my body convulse.

"Ah!" I yelped before reaching down and removing him from the situation. "Get the fuck up here," I told him returning him to my arms.

Settling with his face inches from mine, I stared into his eyes. For a moment, my wolf and I were happy. But the longer I stared, the more I realized that I was fucked. There was no way I was going to be able to hide what I felt for him after this. If someone asked, I wouldn't be able to deny it.

I never knew I could feel like this. And although he didn't know it, he had me wrapped around his delicate little finger.

What was I supposed to do now? What would my father say when he learned that I was falling in love with, not just a man, but the cause of his humiliation?

****Author note: Wondering what would have happened if Kuroi chose the crop? Read the alternate sex scene by becoming a Patron on BookishBoyfriend.com. It's the author's new website where you can have steamy chats with characters from the author's sexy romances. Read the alternate sex scene and try out the steamy chat for free. And don't worry, the chats only get NSFW if you want them to. ☺ Click here to go there now.*

Chapter 9

Kuroi

Ever since the age of 14 when my father gave me to a business partner as a signing bonus, I've had problems sleeping. It started off as not being able to stay asleep. I was never able to figure out why, but I've narrowed it down to two things. Either it was because I was sleeping in a new bed, or because I was woken up every night by an old man pushing his cock into my ass. It remains a mystery.

However, the real problem began when I was not only unable to stay asleep, but I couldn't fall asleep in the first place. There would be multiple days in a row when I wouldn't sleep at all.

I have to admit that it would make me a little crazy. By day three, you did not want to be around me. Ever try to put on makeup while being drunk from exhaustion? It wasn't a good look.

But even after my father's business partner died suddenly and I returned home, I still couldn't sleep. I would go to bars until sunrise, drink all night, and marathon fuck trying to tire myself out. Nothing worked.

Eventually, I just accepted it. I was a bad sleeper whose lovers would always end up dead. Were those two things related? I mean, how could they not be, right?

I certainly don't remember killing any of them. I might have thought about it. Especially the first one. But, all that trouble of making a plan and sticking to it? That's a lot of work. And, luckily, my problems have always ended up taking care of themselves.

Unfortunately, my new problem quickly became that even the ones I wanted to live, died. And it wasn't like I would stab them in my sleep. That would have been easier to accept. No, I would simply be with someone long enough to finally fall asleep in their arms and within weeks, I would be burying them.

And they weren't all old. One of them was 25. If it were still possible for me to love someone, it would have been him. He was everything that my young heart wanted. And in spite of his better judgment, he loved me. Oh well!

I say this to say that never before have I slept in anyone's arms as easily as I slept in Dante's. One explanation could be that Dante keeps drugging me, that bastard. But I'm not waking up with the same ear ringing that I did when I was a kid. So, unless they've come up with better drugs since then, I can't explain it.

In either case, I've learned that being able to fall asleep in Dante's arms came with its own set of problems. For one, I've developed this crazy urge to smother him in his sleep. Don't get me wrong, I don't want to kill him. I just want to make it so I never have to hear him tell me that we have to sleep apart.

I can hear you now, 'Oh Kuroi, that's so extreme. Oh Kuroi, if you kill him, you'll have to live the rest of your life knowing that you couldn't open your throat wide enough to swallow his huge, sigh, HUGE cock.' And you wouldn't be wrong.

But, imagine how it would feel to go 13 years without a good night's sleep, finally get it, and then have it taken away from you. You would smother someone in their sleep too. You would find thicker and thicker vegetables to loosen your throat, show his flag pole who's boss, and then smother him in his sleep just like the rest of us would.

Until then, though, I had to prevent myself from doing anything crazy.

"Hey," Dante said, waking up finding me staring into his eyes from inches away.

"Hey," I crooned feeling more rested than I had in my adult life.

After staring at me for a second, he looked down and lifted my arm. I think he was just trying to lift his own arm, but considering I had handcuffed his wrist to mine, it was a package deal.

"What's up with this?" he asked still trying to wake up.

"What do you mean?" I replied knowing he could have been asking about a number of things.

"The handcuffs. Did you handcuff us together?"

"Why do you ask?"

"Because we're handcuffed together," he explained.

"Oh!"

He looked at me strangely. "So, did you?"

"I've done so many things. You can't expect me to remember all of them," I replied doing my best not to express how silly his question was.

Looking confused for only a moment more, he quickly relaxed and returned to my eyes.

"You know I'm going to have to leave eventually, right?"

"Of course I know you're going to leave. And you'll be taking me with you."

"Oh is that what this is about? What? You think because you're married to me, you're entitled to help run pack business?" he asked amused.

I laughed. "I am not a working girl."

"So, what? You'll just be cuffed to me for the rest of our lives like some sort of ball and…"

"If you call me your ball and chain, I will have to murder you. Which would be a shame considering what we did last night."

Dante smiled and twisted my cuffed arm to wrap his arm around me.

"What we did last night, huh?"

"You do remember, don't you? You made me choose a flog and then you whipped me on the balcony with people watching."

"There were people watching?" Dante asked surprised.

I looked at him like he was an idiot.

"You were whipping a naked man on the balcony of your high rise in the middle of New York City. There was practically a crowd. The only reason a cop didn't show up was because they probably thought you caught me trying to escape."

Dante's head snapped back. "That's not funny."

"We're in America. Trust me, it's a little funny," I reassured him.

For whatever reason, that was what triggered him to try to get up.

"Uncuff me. I need to get ready for work."

"No!" I refused surprised he would ask.

"I'm serious, uncuff me."

"How can I? They're your cuffs. I don't even have the key."

Dante looked at me frustrated and then climbed over me for the nightstand. Opening the drawer, he looked through it.

"Where's the key? I left it in here last night when I set things up."

"Wait, are you saying I wasn't supposed to swallow that?"

Dante rolled back and stared at me.

"What are you, twelve?"

"We're as old as we feel," I told him cheerfully.

Instead of settling in for a relaxing day in bed, my brutish husband snarled, rolled over me, and then tossed me onto his shoulder like a bag of rice.

"What are you doing?" I protested.

"I told you. I've gotta get ready for work. Did you think your childish prank was gonna stop me?"

"Put me down. Who do you think you are?"

"Someone who's gonna tan that hide if you keep messing around like this."

"Now I'm confused. Do you want me to stop messing around or keep messing around?"

"You keep going and you'll find out."

In spite of his very clear promise, I did not find out. I did find out how it felt to shower while thrown over someone's shoulder. And I also found out what it was like watching him shave upside down. But when he really wanted to leave, he did what he had done the night before and broke the cuff off of his wrist.

"Breakaway," he explained.

"Ahh!" I said heartbroken.

"I don't want to see you in my office today."

"Like saying that would ever stop me."

"I'm serious. I can't think when you're around. And I need to figure out what I'm gonna do with Matteo."

I perked up. "I told you, arrange for us to have dinner and I'll find out if he was the one who shot you."

"I don't know, Kuroi. You both can be…"

"Choose your words wisely, husband," I threatened.

"Impulsive."

"You really think I would crawl across the table and slit his throat in a public place for trying to kill you? I mean, I had fun last night but you weren't that good."

"I'm hurt."

"And I'm lying. Last night was great. I would totally slit his throat in a public place for trying to kill you," I said with a smile.

"That's my guy. But still, he's my brother. Whatever he did, I can't let you hurt him like that."

"Fine, I won't slit his throat."

Dante looked at me amused. "You promise?"

"What if I did it with a butter knife? Do you know how hard that would be? I feel like that shouldn't count."

"See, this is why I can't put you two together."

"I'm kidding. As my husband, you should know that I'm very funny."

Dante laughed.

"Yes, you are."

"So, are you going to set up the dinner?"

"I'll set it up for tonight."

"Yay!" I exclaimed actually excited.

"I'll see you later," he said about to leave.

"Uh, uh, uh," I told him stopping him in his tracks.

"What?"

I puckered my lips and pointed at them. I wasn't sure how he would respond to this. Last night he seemed completely into kissing. But a lot of closet-cases like him wanted one thing when the sun was down and another when the sun was up.

To my surprise, Dante released a frustrated exhale, crossed the room and kissed me on the lips. He had tried to make it just a peck, but with him so close, I rested my forearms on his shoulders and got comfortable.

God was he a good kisser. When his tongue touched mine, I felt drunk. My brain melted like warm caramel. And after I had completely lost track of time, he pulled away.

"No, we can't do this now. I really gotta get to work."

"Are you sure?" I asked. "My ass is right here," I told him tilting my naked hole towards him.

Staring at it for a second, it didn't take long for him to break my spell and head out.

"You're not good for me," he said with a smile as the elevator doors closed.

"But you're great for me," I said to myself wondering how I would breathe without him.

With him gone, I fell on the couch staring at the elevator hoping to see it open again. It didn't. Even after I knew it wouldn't, I couldn't get myself to leave thinking that it might. If it wasn't for having to go to the bathroom, I could have stayed there forever.

Once relieved and in the bathroom, I got ready for the day. What would I do with myself considering Dante didn't want me to come to his work? There was a lot of time before our dinner with Matteo. How I filled it would determine what I was going to wear.

Deciding to visit my sister, I put on a midnight blue satin suit with long-cut bell bottom flares. I had the perfect heels for them. And since I would be going home, the makeup would be minimal.

Dressed and ready to go, I soon realized that I didn't have a way of getting there. Retrieving my phone, I gave my husband a call.

"How'd you get this number?" he asked when he answered.

"How did you know it was me?"

"Fair enough. What's up?"

"How do I call for a helicopter?"

"What?"

"When I was home, I called my father's assistant and the pilot would meet me on the heliport. How do you do it? Do I call your assistant?"

Dante laughed. "If you asked my assistant to arrange for the family helicopter, she wouldn't know what the hell you were talking about."

"Do I call your pilot directly?" I asked confused.

"What makes you think that I have a helicopter on standby?"

"Why wouldn't you?"

"Why would I?"

Seeing that this conversation was going nowhere, I got to the point.

"I want to go visit Yuki who is at home today. How do I do it?"

"You could drive."

"Nope. Try again."

"What do you mean, nope?"

"Do I have to explain what no means? Try again!"

"I could have a driver pick you up."

"Nope. Again."

"How about I arrange for a helicopter to take you to Sato's?"

I smiled delighted. "There you go, husband. I knew you'd get it."

Dante didn't seem happy about it, but he informed me that his assistant would be calling me with the details. Within 20 minutes she had, and at the heliport 20 minutes after that, I landed at my father's compound within the hour.

Like every good Japanese, Yuki was a creature of habit. This was the time for her to be in her garden. Finding her there, I regretted wearing heels.

"I can't understand how you could enjoy being out here," I said furious that not even this tinted her porcelain complexion.

"It relaxes me. Perhaps you should consider gardening," she said continuing to prune her winter rose bushes.

"I have my own ways of relaxing," I told my icy sister.

"I imagine."

"I'm sure you don't."

Silence fell between us leaving me staring at her with nothing better to do.

"I bought you a gift."

"Did you?" I asked intrigued. "Will this one be my wedding present?"

"You can think of it however you'd like. Has married life been treating you well?"

Had married life been treating me well? Let's see. I was sleeping better than I have in years. I had had the greatest fuck of my life. And I was beginning to enjoy my husband's company.

"I can think of worse things."

Hearing my declaration, Yuki almost collapsed in surprise… or at least, her version of it, which consisted of a slight glance back with eye contact. Returning her attention to her roses, she said, "I'm pleased."

Pruning for barely a minute more, she gathered her stuff and led me back inside. As she did, she almost expressed an emotion. I had never seen my sister so rattled. Who was this person beside me?

"Tea?" she asked, her tone screaming her distress.

"Please," I replied willing to agree to anything to calm her down.

Having chosen the balcony where I had married Dante for our tea, I understood the cause of my sister's riotous turmoil. It was losing me.

Her delicate heart struggled to handle it. Her expressionless gaze into the woods in front of us was all she could do to not throw herself over the balcony to her death. My heart broke for her.

Yuki, like so many others in my life, was obsessed with me. The men, the women… I didn't want to act like an asshole, but it was the only thing I could do to keep everyone at bay.

It wouldn't surprise me if this was the reason I was given away so young. Because not even my father could resist my seductive power. So sad.

How lucky am I to have inherited my father's curse and to have attracted a spider demon? My unlucky sister attracted what my father tells people I am, a simply house spirt. So she's cursed to bring luck and prosperity to anyone who loves her, while I get to kill anyone who loves me. Seriously, how did I get so lucky?

"You said you had a gift for me?" I asked hoping to rescue my sister from her jealous despair.

Turning back to me, she stared and then got up.

"I will retrieve it."

While she was gone, I allowed my mind to shift to the time I had spent at this compound. I had tried to be here as little as I could. I had always considered it a prison. Living with my lovers had been my escape.

Yuki had never had such options. I wasn't sure if she had even ever had a boyfriend.

It was possible that she had. Over the years I had been gone a lot. Whenever the chance at a new life presented itself, I took it. And as I engaged in another doomed affair, my sister remained here being my father's perfect daughter.

If Yuki ever considered this place her prison, it certainly came with privileges. Unlike me, she had full access to my father's money. And a few times a year she would travel back to Japan to spend time with the brothers I had barely met.

But, even with that freedom, there would always come a time when her leash drew her back. Yuki was the one constant of this compound. She walked the grounds like a porcelain ghost. If she had ever had a lover, it would have had to have been as she traveled. But it was hard to imagine that.

Returning to our tea, Yuki held an elegantly wrapped box. Standing to accept her gift, I held the other end of it and bowed.

"For your happiness," she wished.

"You honor me," I replied unable to ignore my programming. "Please, sit," I said waiting for her to return to her seat.

Again seated with the gift between us, I looked at it with anticipation. Removing the tape while making sure to admire the wrapping, I eventually found a white box. Lifting the top, inside I found what I often had, an elegantly tailored black dress.

I was delighted. If nothing else, Yuki had exquisite taste. Where she found her gifts, I would never know. The lack of a label on them once led me to believe that she had designed them herself. But as they became more elaborate, her having designed them became less likely.

"This is incredible," I said holding it out in front of me.

The top of the dress was sleeveless and form fitting with black threaded embroidery. It was classically Chinese. The bottom continued with the thick black silk which split into pant legs that fell together to resemble a dress.

"I'm glad you like it," Yuki said with the slightest hint of a smile.

"I more than like it. I will be wearing it tonight."

"Will you be going out?"

"I will be having dinner with Dante and his brother," I said proudly.

"Oh."

"Have you met Dante's brother, Matteo?"

Yuki lowered her head and gave a slight twist indicating she hadn't.

"Someone made an attempt on Dante's life."

"Oh?"

"It was why he had crashed the car on our wedding day. He hadn't just run into a tree trying to get away from me," I said trying to hide the relief I felt saying it.

"Huh," she chirped ignoring my emotional indulgence. "And your dinner with Matteo?"

"He believes there was someone waiting for him outside our compound who took a shot at him."

"Does father know about this?"

"He knows none of this. And you must be sworn to secrecy. Until we figure out who tried to kill him, this can't get out."

"Your secrets have always been safe with me."

"I know," I said glancing down at the dress.

Yuki might have known my secrets before I had. She had bought me my first dress before I had tried one on. Staring at her first gift, I hadn't known what to think. I had felt both exposed and humiliated. But the joy she expressed when I tried it on was what made it comfortable.

Now, my dresses were as much a part of me as any of my clothing. It was my way of expressing who I was. It had been my rebellion while under my father's strong thumb, and a way of throwing off my enemies. How were they supposed to respond to someone who looked like me knowing the wrong word could be their last?

"Why is it that your husband suspects his brother?"

"They think he was ordered to by their father."

"And you are joining them for dinner tonight?"

"I told Dante that I would be able to see his guilt."

"Have you gained a power I am unaware of?" she asked teasing me.

"I have gained many," I replied jokingly. "I can now see through walls."

"That is great skill."

"I can also move the saucer from under the cup without touching it," I told her holding my hands above it as if about to levitate it. "I just don't want to right now," I said relaxing in mock refusal.

Yuki put her hand over her mouth hiding her laughter. It always made me feel good to make my sister laugh. It had never been easy. But when I did, I felt complete.

Enjoying the rest of the day with my sister, I left her promising that I would visit again. And I did plan to in spite of all of her emotional outbursts.

Calling Dante's assistant, the helicopter was there with enough time to return home, shower again and get dressed for dinner. I knew what I would wear, but I hadn't decided on the makeup. What impression did I want to make on my new brother?

He certainly needed to know that I would kill him if he went after Dante. What would communicate that? Cat eyes were so out of fashion that someone would have to be crazy to wear it. Was I that type of crazy? Or would that be going too far?

Deciding on a pale foundation that would give me a ghostly look, I emphasized my already thick eyebrows and chose black lipstick. It was very 1980s Grace Jones. It said, don't turn your back on me because I'm crazy enough to have sex with O.J. Simpson.

"What the fuck?" Dante said when he came to change and get me. "You know that we're having dinner with my brother, right? He's not gonna go for any of this shit you're wearing."

As Dante waved indicating everything about me, I ignored him.

"Well, the purpose of tonight isn't to have him go for me. It is to find out if he tried to kill you."

"Yeah, but if he didn't, you're gonna have to see him on a regular basis. Matteo isn't as open minded as I am."

"Then he's going to have to learn to be, isn't he."

Dante looked flustered. I didn't think it possible for someone with so many tattoos. Taking my hand, he said, "I want you to know that you look fuckin' great right now. I'm serious. I love everything about it. But when it comes to members of my pack…"

"When it comes to members of your pack, they'll have to get used to it."

"Kuroi…"

"Are you asking me to stab you again?"

Dante let go of my hand and jumped back.

"No!" When he saw I wasn't going to, he added, "I'm still healing from the last time."

Remembering what I had done to him. I did feel a little bad.

"Ahhh, my poor baby," I said approaching him slowly.

Directly in front of him, I slipped my hand on his side and with my thumb, lightly brushed the spot where I stabbed him. Dante's body was tense beneath me, but he didn't pull away.

"I will never let anyone do this to you again," I told him looking up into his eyes.

"You're the one who did it. Are you gonna do it again?"

"I hope not," I told him honestly. "I only want to protect you."

Dante seemed less assured by my answer than I wanted him to be. That was probably because I didn't want to lie to him. I still didn't know what I did when I slept. He should be ready to defend himself if in exhausted delusion I tried something.

I truly didn't want to hurt him again. But I wasn't sure I could stop myself. I could never be trusted.

"You should get ready," I told him not wanting to let him go.

He stared down at me before moving.

"If you are good tonight, maybe I'll have something waiting for you when we get home."

"Don't make a promise you can't keep," I replied flirtatiously.

"You can take me at my word. Always," he told me squeezing my ass.

Feeling his large hand consume me, my cock got hard. What did he have in mind? I had liked everything about what we had done the night before. The only downside was that I couldn't also feel the crop.

"I'll be good," I said pressing where I stabbed him with my thumb.

He flinched tightening his grip on my ass. His fingers dug into me almost tearing into my flesh. It hurt and I liked it.

With his free hand shooting to my wrist to remove it from his side, I gave another small squeeze and let go. Once my hand was off of him, he leaned down and gave me a kiss. It wasn't long enough, but it reminded me of the benefits of being good.

Perhaps I wasn't going to jump across the table and slit Matteo's throat after all. I had too much to lose if I did. Did my husband already know how to control me? I didn't know how I felt about that.

When Dante left me to get ready. I remained in the living room waiting for him. When he returned, it was with a surprise. He looked different. Everything he wore was basically the same but his button-up dress shirt was striped with red, white, and blue. Was this my husband relaxing? It might have been.

Heading to the elevator, I took his arm. When I had it, he didn't resist. He stood up straighter. It was like he enjoyed having me by his side. I couldn't believe that because no one did. Even the boy I had loved shied away from allowing us to be seen in public together.

He wasn't a part of the world Dante and I shared, so he feared for his life. Turns out, he had a right to be. He simply feared the wrong people. He should have feared the only person he trusted. Talk about a bad judge of character.

Arriving at the restaurant, I waited for Dante to open my car door. It took him a second to realize what I was doing, but he figured it out.

"Don't expect me to do this every time," he informed me as I got out.

I ignored him, waited for him to close the car door, and then took his arm. Again, he straightened his back and walked taller.

Entering the restaurant, I scanned the room. Making note of the exits, I next examined the patrons. There was a mix of clientele none of which were Asian or black.

There was one person looking at us, though. He was hard to miss. He looked like a prettier version of Dante. And if I were single and looking to get fucked tonight, he would be who I left with.

"Your brother is gay?" I asked Dante whose attention snapped to me in surprise.

"Not in a million years," he said confidently.

I looked back at the man who watched us approach. I could see the wheels in his head spinning. He was confused about how to respond. Seeing us had unbalanced him. That was good. Now I had to continue it.

"Do you know who I am?" I said to Matteo before Dante got a chance to speak.

"I've heard a lot about you," Matteo said with a smile.

"All of it good, I'm sure," I told him.

"Depends. Is what they say true?"

"And what do they say?" I said as my jaw clenched.

"How about you two wait until we sit down before making a scene," Dante said looking uneasy.

"Who's making a scene?" I asked as Dante pulled out my chair for me.

"You two. And that's not how this fuckin' night is gonna go."

I looked at Dante amused.

"And how is tonight going to go?"

Dante sat.

"It's gonna start with me introducing you two."

"Then go ahead. Introduce us," I said cutting him off.

Dante adjusted in his chair uncomfortably.

"Kuroi, this is my brother, Matteo. Matteo, this is… ah"

"His husband," I said cutting him off again. "I'm his husband," I said reaching across the table and shaking Matteo's hand. "It seems like we have something in common," I told him with a smile.

"Yeah? What's that?" Matteo asked.

"Kuroi!" Dante said reading my mind.

I turned to Dante and relented with a shrug.

"What do we have in common?" he asked, his eyes bouncing between Dante and me.

"Me. I'm what you have in common," Dante replied.

"Yeah. Guess so," Matteo agreed relaxing.

As I stared at him watching his every move, he stared back at me. He was definitely gay.

"So, you're the famous spider demon," he said with a smile.

Every muscle in my body tensed hearing him say it. I had killed people for less.

"Does everyone you sleep with die?" Matteo asked amused. "Should I worry about my brother?"

"What the fuck are you askin'?" Dante interjected.

"I'm asking if the two of you are fuckin'," he said bluntly.

I replied, "I'm his husband. What do you think?"

Matteo fell back in his seat and laughed.

"What are you laughing at? Jealous?" I challenged.

"Maybe. What makes an ass so good it could turn my brother?"

"Watch your fuckin' mouth, Matteo."

"I'm just saying, there's got to be something really good under there if it could turn you gay. Maybe you should spread the love," Matteo said gesturing to me.

That was when Dante jumped up, reached across the table, grabbed a knife and pressed it to his brother throat.

"I said watch your fuckin' mouth. You understand me?"

Not getting what was going on, Matteo laughed.

"Alright. I got it. I'll watch what I say."

When Dante didn't move, I added, "I think he gets it."

"I get it, Dante. I get it," he said holding up his hands.

It took a second, but Dante relaxed. I looked around at the people who had stopped to stare at us.

"He thought he was choking," I told everyone watching us. "False alarm. You are dismissed."

Eventually everyone returned to their meal and everyone at our table relaxed.

"So, I hear that you are the one responsible for Dante and my marriage," I asked refocusing on why we had come.

"And it looks like you two should be thanking me," he said proudly.

"You think anything that happens between Kuroi and me lets you off the hook for the crazy shit you pulled?"

"You know why I did it, Dante," Matteo said defensively.

"Why did you do it?" I asked curiously.

Matteo turned to me.

"Because that fucker messed up my friend's little sister," Matteo said immediately angered.

"Messed up how?"

"Messed up in the way that gets you killed," Matteo explained. "You should know something about that."

"So, you're saying he deserved it?"

"He was practically asking for it."

"Is that why you took a shot at Dante? Was he asking for it too?"

"What are you talking about? Who took a shot at you?" Matteo asked his brother.

"Don't play dumb. We know you took a shot at him," I continued.

"What the fuck is he talking about, Dante?"

A reluctant Dante leaned forward with his elbows on the table and said, "I think what Kuroi is trying to ask you is, where were you when I went to Sato's? Did you follow me up there?"

"Follow you up there? Why would I follow you up there?"

"To take a shot at me when I was leaving."

"To take a shot at you? Why would I try to shoot you?" he asked confused.

"Maybe you were ordered to," Dante suggested.

Matteo stared at Dante not answering.

"Pa didn't ask me to take you out," he replied soberly.

Sensing that there was more to his story like I did, Dante asked, "What did he ask you to do?"

Matteo looked down unable to maintain eye contact with either of us.

"Ya know, you shouldn't have cut Pa out like you did. He doesn't like it."

"What did he ask you to do, Matteo?"

"He didn't ask me to do anything," he said still not looking up.

"Fuckin' talk to me, Matteo," Dante demanded. "What aren't you telling me?"

"It's just that, Pa's been asking if I would treat the business like you do."

"What does that mean?"

"You know Pa. He doesn't like change. He's been doing things the same way since he was born. You came in, made all of these changes, and blocked him out. He wants back in."

"He wants to know who you would back if he pushed me out."

"More like, if you were out of the picture. He asked me how I would run the pack."

"You think he's gonna make a move against me," Dante clarified.

Matteo looked at his brother. "I think he already has."

"How's that?" Dante asked laser-focused.

"Uncle Vinny's back."

Dante slowly fell into his chair hearing the news. I looked between the two of them trying to figure out what was going on.

"Who's Uncle Vinny?"

Matteo replied, "He's our father's brother. Legend has it that he once made a move against our father for the pack and my father exiled him for it. He's been asking to return to the States for thirty years and our father wouldn't let him."

"And you think that your father letting him come back has to do with him making a move against Dante?" I clarified.

Matteo looked at Dante for confirmation. "Why would he change his mind now after thirty years?"

"Why are you telling me this? You could've held this back," Dante asked Matteo.

"I'm telling you because you're my brother. You've always had my back. I want you to know that I have yours. More than being my alpha, we're family. There's nothing that will come between us no matter how tight their ass is."

Dante turned his attention to me for my response. For once, I didn't know what to say.

Matteo was telling Dante that I shouldn't matter. Did Dante believe that? Did I matter to him or was I just a diversion? Maybe all of my makeup had tricked him into believing that he was with a woman and it was just a matter of time before he realized what I was.

With a scared waiter approaching the table soon afterwards, Dante didn't address what Matteo had suggested. Instead, we ordered Italian pasta and wine, and pretended Matteo hadn't said anything he had.

Droning on about a tattoo artist he had heard about in Los Angeles, Matteo had a hard time looking me in the eyes. After dinner when Dante headed to the bathroom, Matteo turned to me.

"I don't know what you and Sato have planned. But if you touch a hair on my brother's head, I'll skin you like a goat."

"Do you think you could stop me if we did have something planned?"

"How about I stop you now and not have to worry about it?"

With his hand under the table, I heard the click as his gun's safety unlock.

Knowing that there was nothing I could do to get away at this range, I asked him, "Do you think Dante would ever forgive you if you did that?"

"Dante's forgiven me for all kinds of shit. What's one more thing?"

As much as I didn't like it, Matteo had me. Trapped on the other side of the table, there was no way to get up before he could get off two shots.

"I am not my father's assassin. Are you?"

"Maybe Sato knows he doesn't have to ask you."

As much as I hated it, Matteo was right. Every man I've been with for more than a night, has died. If my father wanted someone dead, all he had to do was get me to love them. Without asking for it, they would be out of the picture.

"If you believe that, then shoot," I told him resigned to my fate. "Go ahead. Do it."

"What's going on?" Dante asked returning to the table with Matteo and me staring coldly at each other.

Matteo's arm holding the gun, retreated.

"I was just welcoming my new brother-in-law to the family."

"Was he?" Dante asked me.

"I've never felt more at home," I said not taking my eyes off Matteo.

As much as I didn't want to admit it, Matteo had gotten into my head.

"I don't think he shot at you," I told Dante on the car ride home.

"I don't think so either. And if what he said about Uncle Vinny is true, and he is back, we have another problem."

"Sounds like it," I agreed.

"You okay, Kuroi? You've been quiet since I got back from the bathroom," he asked after I continued not to be able to look him in the eyes.

"I'm fine."

"You don't seem fine."

"I'm tired."

"Are you too tired to collect your reward for being good tonight?"

I turned to see the smirk on his beautiful face.

"Yeah. Maybe another night."

"Oh. Yea, of course," he said quickly retreating.

I wanted to explain to him that it was a bad idea to let me get close to him. I couldn't be trusted. He had to know that. If I allowed myself to fall for him, he would end up dead. I was the spider demon. That's all I would ever be.

Parking, we ascended the elevators to our place. We didn't touch. When the doors opened, I headed to the guest room.

"Where you goin'?" he asked as I crossed the room.

"To bed."

"Aren't you gonna join me?"

"Maybe it's not such a good idea."

"If Matteo said something to you, I swear to God, I'll ring his fuckin' neck."

I looked back hoping to calm him.

"He didn't say anything to me that wasn't true."

"I'll fuckin' kill him."

"No, Dante. It's not about him. It's about me. I don't want to hurt you."

"You've already had the chance. You didn't. You're not gonna hurt me."

"You don't know that. And the reason that you don't is because I don't know it."

"Kuroi," Dante said approaching me and encircling my biceps with his large hands.

"No, Dante. I kill people."

"You won't kill me."

"I kill the people I love. You don't want me to love you. Let me go, Dante," I told him soberly.

Dante let go of my arms and I walked away. When I was alone in the guest bedroom with the door closed, I sat on the bed, lowered my face into my hands, and I cried.

Chapter 10

Dante

I was gonna kill Matteo for whatever he said to Kuroi. Until I had left for the bathroom, everything had gone well. Yeah, I had found out that my father had invited his treacherous brother back into our lives so he could kill me. But Matteo and Kuroi had been getting along.

What could Matteo have said to him? I had never seen Kuroi like this. It was like he was a different person. I wanted the Kuroi I knew back.

Hoping all he needed was a good night's sleep, I headed to my room and bed. Remembering the feeling of Kuroi in my arms, I couldn't fall asleep. By morning, I had slept three hours at most. And when I returned to the living room to find the guest bedroom door still closed, I wasn't sure what to do.

"Are you up?" I asked knocking on his door. "Kuroi?"

"What?" I heard him say from within.

"I need your help. Can I come in?"

"It's your house," he said not sounding good.

Entering, I found what he was wearing the night before on the floor while his pillows were smeared with makeup. I hadn't known Kuroi long, but this didn't seem like him. Looking down at him as he buried his face into his pillow, I said, "I could use your expertise today."

"What is it?"

"I need to find my Uncle Vinny. If he's in town, I'm gonna need some back up."

"Why don't you ask Matteo?"

"I don't trust Matteo with this. I trust you."

"You shouldn't."

"Like you said, you kill people. And if it came down to it, I need someone who won't hesitate out of family loyalty."

What I had said was true, wasn't it? Uncle Vinny was family even if he wasn't a member of our pack. Both Matteo and Lorenzo could hesitate if things went south. Kuroi wouldn't. He really was the only person I could trust to have my back.

"Come on, Kuroi, I need you."

Kuroi turned to look at me.

"I'm serious. You're the only one I can trust with this," I told him sincerely.

Kuroi looked down, wiped his face on his pillow and then got up.

"Fine. Give me a few minutes to get dressed."

Returning to the living room, I learned what my new husband meant when he requested "a few minutes". Forty minutes later, he emerged looking more like himself.

"You took your sweet time," I said failing to hide how annoyed I was.

"You wanted my help, didn't you? I had to put myself on."

He spoke as if the person I knew as Kuroi was just a mask he wore. Was it? How much did I know about Kuroi? How much could I know about him? I hadn't known him that long.

"Coffee? I made a pot," I told him as I held up my mug.

Kuroi poured coffee into a to-go mug and we headed out.

"So, what's the plan?" He asked me on the drive to the office.

"We'll meet with Lorenzo."

"Are you sure you can trust him?"

"If I can't, we're in deep shit. Because he knows everything."

"Everything?" Kuroi asked me suggestively.

"Well, there are a few things he doesn't know. But he knows a lot."

Kuroi didn't reply to that. I couldn't tell what he was thinking, but the more we talked, the more my Kuroi reemerged. Wait, when did I start thinking of him as 'My Kuroi'?

That was what he was though, mine. And if anyone tried to get between us like Matteo had, they were gonna have to deal with me. My brother was going to have to learn that. But first, we were gonna have to deal with my father and his attempt to get rid of me.

Arriving at my office later than usual, I found Lorenzo already there. Sitting in the chair in front of my desk, he did a double-take when I walked in with Kuroi. With his eyes locked on Kuroi, he asked me,

"How did things go last night with Matteo?"

As I settled behind my desk, Kuroi took the club chair next to the window. Although he had worn a man's suit, I spotted his heels as he put his feet on the coffee table. They looked like thigh high boots that would make him three inches taller.

"It was educational," I told Lorenzo checking my calendar for the day.

"Don't leave me in suspense. Was it him who took a shot at you?"

"I don't think it was."

"Then who?"

"Did you know Uncle Vinny was in town?" I said watching Lorenzo closely for deception.

"Uncle Vinny?" Lorenzo asked surprised. "Since when?"

"Don't know. But if he's back, there's gotta be a reason. He's been persona non grata with Pa our entire lives. Now Pa's pissed at me for getting married and Uncle Vinny's back?"

"This is Pa's move," Lorenzo said realizing it.

"That's what Matteo thinks."

"So, what are you gonna do?"

"We gotta find him and figure out why he's here."

"And if he's here to do Pa's dirty work?"

"We eliminate him."

"We?" Lorenzo asked losing a shade of color from his face. As dangerous as Lorenzo was, his wolf had never killed anyone. There was a part of me that liked that. Having blood on your hands wasn't a badge of honor. It was a necessary evil.

If I could protect my little brother from that, I would. It was the least I could do. Growing up the way we did, there were certain things that were unavoidable. Prey needs to know how to survive among predators. But watching as the light went out in someone's eyes wasn't anything Lorenzo needed to experience.

"Kuroi and me," I clarified.

"You and Kuroi?" he said looking back at my husband.

"Yeah. This is family matters. I'm keeping it in the family," I said sending a message to Lorenzo about who Kuroi was to me.

"Got it. So, do you know for sure that he's in town?"

"We haven't gotten that far yet," I explained.

"I can find out," Kuroi said to my surprise.

"You? How? You don't know anything about him," I asked my deathly calm husband.

"I don't need to. All I need is his name. Which is?"

"Vincent Ricco."

"Give me to the end of the day," Kuroi said before getting up and walking out.

When he was gone, Lorenzo turned back to me and lowered his voice.

"Are you sure you can trust him, Dante?"

"Who Kuroi?"

"Who the fuck do you think I mean?" he snapped.

I stared at him not liking the way he raised his voice.

"Sorry, Dante. But yeah, Kuroi. Think about it. They call him the spider demon. Everyone he's with dies. Everyone!"

"That's another thing. I don't want to hear any more about that spider demon shit."

"You don't want to hear any more about it? Dante, you married him and immediately almost died. Do you think that was a coincidence?"

"Do I think that marrying Kuroi pissed Pa off enough to try and kill me?"

"But that's the thing. Let's just say that it was Matteo who shot you. How did it go down?"

"What do you mean?"

Lorenzo got up and walked around the room as he thought.

"Okay, you're saying that when we drove up there, your plan was to talk Sato out of the deal, right?"

"Right."

"So, there was no way you could know that he was planning on marrying you right then. And if you didn't know, Pa definitely didn't know. So, why would he have Matteo follow you with a sharpshooter rifle in case you did something to piss him off?"

"I don't know. Our father is fucked up," I explained.

"He's fucked up. But what's the reason you needed to take control of the business?"

"Because he's not strategic," I realized.

"Exactly. And it would require some strategic thinking to be that many steps ahead. I could do it. You might be able to do it. But Pa and Matteo…?"

I had to admit that Lorenzo was right. I was giving Pa a lot more credit than he deserved. Yeah, Matteo might be the only one capable of making that shot. But why would he have been there to take it?

"What are you suggesting, that I made up getting shot?"

"I'm not suggesting you made up anything. But, what if the feeling in your neck wasn't what you think it was?"

"What else could it be?"

"It could be a random nerve pinch. It could be a phantom pain. I get them all of the time. For no reason, something will hurt, then it goes away."

"So, you think it was all in my head?"

"What I'm saying is that the most obvious answer is usually the correct one. There is only one person capable of making a shot like that and there was no reason for him to be there. That leaves the kiss from the spider demon being the most likely cause of your crash."

"I told you to stop with that spider demon shit."

"Then you give me another explanation. You're there. He kisses you. Less than five minutes later you're driving into a tree. What else could possibly have happened?"

I turned my attention out the window knowing there was one other thing.

"What is it?" Lorenzo asked, always the perceptive one.

"When I was in the hospital, the doctor, Sato's doctor I'll add, she had this crazy idea that it could be something else."

Lorenzo tilted his head like a dog hearing something it's never heard before.

"The doctor suggested that it wasn't an attack on my life. She thought it was…" I paused trying to think of a reason I shouldn't say it. I couldn't come up with one. "…A panic attack."

Lorenzo stared at me speechless. I could see his mind working.

"No," he concluded as confidently as he had said anything.

"And that's what I said. Of course it wasn't a panic attack. I don't get fuckin' panic attacks."

"You don't."

I stared at Lorenzo's unwavering confidence in me.

"Right. But, how would you know that?" I asked curiously.

"What do you mean, how? I know you."

"You don't know everything about me."

"Are you talking about how you sometimes fuck guys?"

"Watch your fuckin' mouth," I said reverting back to my pre-Kuroi response.

"You married a fuckin' man. I think you can admit that you've fucked guys before. What? You think I've never done it? You think Matteo hasn't?"

"What?" I asked stunned.

"All I'm saying is, I know you. Even when you think I didn't, I did. And I'm telling you, it wasn't a panic attack."

I fell back in my chair dumbstruck. For years I had hidden the things I was doing. How long had he known? Who else knew?

"Who else have you told?" I asked ashamed.

"What? About what you do in the privacy of your bedroom that has nothing to do with the pack or anything else?"

"Yeah. You seemed to not have a problem telling me about Matteo."

"I also told you about myself. You're not gonna ask me about that?"

"The guy in the hallway that night when I came over. He was coming from your place. That's why you had enough food for two people."

Lorenzo shook his head in acknowledgement.

"How long have you been with him?"

"Not long. I wouldn't call it anything serious. Our world is a lot to put on someone who has no idea what they're getting into."

"Then you get it."

"You mean, why it is that you're blind to Kuroi trying to kill you?"

"No. I mean, why it's not Kuroi. Think about it. What you feel is what he feels. He's not some fuckin' monster. I get his world. Fuck, I'm a part of it. Why would he try to kill the only man who gets him?"

"Because it's his nature. Spider demon's don't kill because the want to. They do it to survive. Who knows, maybe he loves you. But that's not gonna stop him from eating you after you've given him what he needs."

Chapter 11

Kuroi

When you can't get out of your head, bury your head in your work. I don't know who said it, so I'm claiming it as a Kuroi original.

I wasn't expecting Dante to wake me up this morning. I thought I was giving him what he wanted by getting out of his room. Wasn't that the deal we had made, that I would only be in his room a few times a week?

I had slept there a couple nights in a row. Didn't he want me to give him some space? If he did, why hadn't he just gone to work this morning?

And, he had practically banned me from his office. This morning he invited me to join him? This had to be his way of taunting death. So, if he ended up dead now, wouldn't he have just been asking for it?

Instead of allowing my sleep-deprived brain to spiral on this, I did what I did best. There was someone who needed finding. I had found people before. My father's organization was uniquely equipped for that and I had full access to it.

My first stop was to the woman who the Yakuza had made rich for her services. The foothold my father's organization had been able to secure in New York was heroin import. It sounds dangerous and exciting, but it's actually quite boring.

We weren't responsible for growing or refining it. We didn't even transport it from Afghanistan to the Afghan airport. We simply got it onto cargo planes and cleared it through customs in the United States. Once in, we funneled it to local distributors who were happy to have our services.

The growers and transports thought of us as their wholesalers. The distributors thought of us as their bank. We extended lines of credit to those who couldn't pay up front and they got a set time for repayment. How was this any different from importing rugs?

What this meant was that my father's organization had two specialties, routing money and clearing customs. We had dozens of people we could rely on for each. The person with the information I would need today was our chief customs specialist.

Whether it was product or people, she could get it through U.S. customs. She wasn't the only person in her position that we had access to, but she was the best. Not only could she clear the path through checkpoints for anything we needed, she had access to the national database of everything and everyone entering or leaving the country.

"Vincent Ricci," I told her sitting across from her in her office at the airport.

I liked dealing with her. Unlike so many others, she had no fear. I was told that she grew up in the abandoned subway lines under New York City. She was a mole person.

I could only guess what she saw as a child. But it was enough motivation to claw her way out and never have to live that way again. As far as my father can tell, she doesn't even spend what we pay her. She probably just sleeps on it for security.

That's fine with us. Large purchases were how people in her position got caught. Make a security blanket out of the cash for all we care. We just needed results and she gave it to us.

"Leaving or arriving?" she asked staring at me with her vacant mole person eyes.

"Arriving. We think he's already here."

"For how long?"

"We don't know. Maybe a few days."

She nodded her head and lost herself in the data flashing on the screen.

"The search will take a while."

"Should I wait for it?"

"I would rather you didn't. I'm surprised your father authorized you being here. Your presence could raise questions."

"Just do the search," I demanded knowing she was right.

I drew attention by design. I was also easy to remember. The last thing my father needed was for someone to recognize me as his son and to wonder why I was here talking to who I was.

An hour later, she asked, "Vincent Ricci arriving from Rome, Italy two days ago?"

"That sounds right. Does it say where he'll be staying while in New York?"

With a few more strokes, she had an answer.

"Can you write it down for me?" I asked her eventually receiving it on a slip of paper. "Thank you."

As I got up she stopped me.

"My brother didn't deserve what he got."

Pausing, I looked at her confused. "Your brother?"

"Ricci," she said referring to the name she had written down. "Matteo Ricci killed my brother. He didn't deserve that."

I hadn't made the connection. Her brother was the one Matteo had killed and had dragged behind his car in Yakuza territory.

"He didn't," I agreed.

"They say he went crazy on that Italian girl, but it wasn't his idea."

"What do you mean?"

"Someone told him to do it. Or, at least they put the idea in his head."

"How do you know that?" I asked suddenly intrigued.

"He told me before…" she drifted off unable to acknowledge her brother was gone. "He didn't say who, but someone told him that she liked it rough."

"She would have had to have liked it very rough according to what I heard."

"My brother could get carried away. But I'm telling you, it wasn't his idea. He didn't even know who she was until someone whispered in his ear. Now he's dead. Ricci needs to pay for what he did."

Did she know that my father had collected on the Ricci debt by marrying me to Dante? She had to have known. Who in the organization didn't know? That meant that she was questioning my father's judgment regarding my marriage being enough.

"You really have no fear."

"What is left for me to be afraid of?"

"Me," I told her before leaving her office and closing the door behind me.

Having taken a taxi to the airport, I caught another one back into town. Staring at the address as we drove, I wondered what I should do with it.

Matteo believed that Vincent Ricci was in town to kill Dante. If that was true, he needed to be taught a lesson. But was it true? I didn't know Matteo so I didn't know if what he said could be trusted.

He had pulled a gun on me. If he was willing to kill me to save his brother, that was definitely a plus in my book. I would have done the same thing, only Matteo wouldn't have seen it coming.

Redirecting the taxi to the address on the paper, we pulled into an Italian neighborhood in the Bronx. It was the type of place I imagined Dante growing up. The streets were lined with modest two-story homes with postcard sized yards. And there were more than one stoop with guys wearing white tank tops and gold chains.

The house at the address Vincent Ricci had put on his immigration form looked like every other house on the block. He hadn't included who he would be staying with. But if he was staying here, the person had lived here for a while.

Could it be Vincent's sister? Had Dante mentioned anything about having an aunt? I wasn't sure but Italians were known for having large families. His father had to have more siblings. Dante was one of about five kids. The same had to be true about their father.

What must it have been like growing up in a family like Dante's? I didn't know much about him before our marriage, but the Ricci's were a prominent mafia family in New York. Everyone knew the basics.

Dante was the respected oldest son. Matteo was the psychopath. And the rest of them kept out of the spotlight.

If any of them, I had always imagined ending up with Matteo. Dante was right, though. Ten minutes alone and we would have killed each other. We almost already did.

But looking into Matteo's eyes, I always saw a crazy bisexual looking back. He would be the type to pin you to the bed and fuck you until you lost feeling in your legs. Of course, he might also kill you for suggesting he was gay. So…

Could that be what happened with the chief customs specialist's brother? I don't doubt that it started with Matteo confronting him about what happened with his friend's sister. But no one takes it that far with a made man.

And, he could have just killed him. Instead, he dragged him behind his car rubbing it into my father's face. What could possibly trigger that level of insanity other than gay panic?

What had she said about there being someone who whispered into her brother's ear? What did that mean? If that was true, who would have suggested something like that? And why? Could they know the firestorm it would ignite?

As I sat thinking about it, an older Italian man descended the stairs of the brownstone I was watching.

He was frailer than I pictured Dante's uncle to be. He resembled Lorenzo if any of them. And dressed in a tan suit that wouldn't grab anyone's attention, he stepped onto the sidewalk with a smile on his face and a skip in his step.

This was Vincent Ricci. I had no doubt.

Feeling good about myself, I texted Dante on the way home.

'I've been good. I think I deserve a reward tonight,' I wrote with my skin tingling waiting for a response.

'Have you? Haha. Did you find out something about Uncle Vinny?'

'Treat first. Answers later.'

There was a pause before he replied,

'What do you want?'

'You know what I want.'

I considered replying with a winking emoji but I wasn't in the sixth grade so I didn't. He, however, replied with two emojis, a leather paddle and an open hand. The text that followed read, 'Choose one'.

Heat washed through my body and my heart thumped.

'Both,' I replied.

'Choose one'.

I sent him a single tear emoji.

'Oh, you will. Choose one.'

My cock got so hard it hurt. How was I supposed to choose between the two? I wanted everything he had to give me.

'You said if I was good, I could have both,' I protested.

'CHOOSE ONE,' he replied sending shivers through me.

'Yes, sir,' I wrote slipping out of my rebellious boy mode into that of an obedient submissive.

I still didn't know which I wanted. The thought of his large bare hand stinging my ass made me weak in the knees. But imagining the sound as the leather paddle snapped my ass…

I replied with the paddle emoji.

'I will be home at 6:30. You will be prepared and you will do what you're told.'

My mind swirled with anticipation for what would happen next. I would be home an hour before he would. I had time to prepare. How, though?

Hurrying to the closet in the guest room where I kept my clothes, I fingered through everything until one thing stood out. It was a floor length cloak I had bought when I was feeling particularly dramatic. Designed to encircle the wearer completely, what said obedient submissive better than dressing like a Catholic priest?

Deciding to wear it with nothing underneath and turned to open in the back, that just left my hair and makeup. Staring in the mirror at what I had to work with, all I could see was the devil. But that was off theme. I needed to look like a Catholic school boy or something close.

With only forty minutes left before the night began, I took a shower and washed my hair. That's when it hit me. Dante had never seen me with my bush of hair slicked back. With it, I passed as what I was, Japanese. What could be more obedient and submissive than that?

Using my thickest hair gel, I pushed it through my hair until every curl was gone. Next, I applied mascara until my wide eyes slanted and the creases in my eyelids faded. I wasn't prepared for who I saw in the mirror when I was done.

Kuroi was gone. Sitting before me was the boy my father would have had if not for my mother's blackness. Would my father have loved this version of me? Would he have given this son to his business partners to use and dispose of?

I would never know because this would never be me. But tonight I could pretend. And the boy who stared back in the mirror was ashamed of all of the bad things he's done.

He wanted to be punished. He desperately needed to cleanse his soul so he could be good again. He wanted so badly to be good.

Whipped out of my thoughts by the elevator door opening, I turned toward the bedroom door feeling my chest clench. It wasn't me who would go out there to meet Dante. It was Shiro. I knew how Shiro thought and behaved because it was the opposite of how I would.

Leaving the makeup mirror, I adjusted the cloak around me and approached the closed bedroom door.

"Kuroi?" Dante called in a stern voice.

I took a breath and opened the door.

"Kuroi isn't here. He sent me to take his punishment."

Dante's eyes widened seeing me. He looked confused but only for a moment.

"Did you agree to this, because Kuroi has a lot coming to him?" Dante asked tilting up the paddle that he held by his side.

Past the handle, it was a foot long and three inches wide. All of it was covered in leather. Seeing it, my balls tingled. My breath hitched.

"Yes, sir."

"You will take his punishment for him?"

"I will take everything he has coming," Shiro said bowing his head.

With my head lowered, I couldn't see what Dante was doing.

"Did Kuroi tell you to do whatever I said?"

"Yes, sir. I am to do anything you tell me."

"What is our safe word?"

"Cherries."

"Stand up," he ordered.

I did. Meeting his eyes, I found a glimmer in them that I had never seen before. I wasn't sure what to think. I just knew I wanted more of it.

"Where's your phone?"

"My phone?" I asked caught off guard.

"Or, Kuroi's phone. Where's that?"

"It's…" I looked back at the guest bedroom wondering if I had left it in my pants pocket. "… In there."

"Get it."

Confused where he was going with this, I did what I was told. Taking small steps like the priests did in old kung fu movies, I retrieved my phone and returned. Dante scanned the room.

"Prop it up on the kitchen island. Vertically," he directed.

Following his instructions, I leaned it against the fruit basket getting excited that he wanted to record this.

"Now, bend over so your face fills the screen."

"What?"

"What was that?" Dante asked angered.

"What, sir?"

He calmed.

"You heard me." He repeated it slowly. "Bend over so that your face fills the screen."

I stared at Dante not sure what was going on. My beating heart slammed against my chest. Terror crept into my thoughts, but I did as he said.

With my forearms flat on the counter and my stomach pressed against the edge, my cloak parted revealing my ass. Stepping behind me, he lightly brushed the leather against my naked skin. I thought he was about to let loose when he said,

"Now, facetime your sister," he said in a low, dark voice.

I lay shocked. He couldn't be serious. I wasn't Kuroi. I was Shiro. And Yuki didn't know anything about this side of me. She was naïve and innocent. I couldn't call her like this.

"I said call Kuroi's sister! You know the number, right?"

"Yes, sir," I replied embarrassed for Shiro.

"Kuroi told you to do whatever I told you to, didn't he?"

"Yes, sir."

"Then do as I say and call Yuki now."

I didn't know what was going on, but I did it. I reached forward, called Yuki and prayed that she didn't answer.

"Hello?" She said before jerking back at the sight of Shiro filling the screen.

"Hello, my name is Shiro and I was told to call you."

As soon as I said it, I felt the paddle connect with my bare ass harder than I could have ever imagined. The sound was deafening. Hearing it, Yuki reacted in horror.

I was shocked at what was happening. I was embarrassed. In all of the years I had played these types of games, I had never experienced anything like this. But before I could react, I felt the paddle again.

Hearing the second, this time Yuki was calm. Her stoicism was back.

"Are you being disciplined, Shiro?" she asked as if asking me what I had had for breakfast.

"Yes, ma'am. I am."

Dante let loose again. The sting was so intense my legs danced. Still, my face never left the screen.

"Are you learning to submit to your superiors?" she asked taking a harsher tone.

"Yes, ma'am. I am."

Dante struck again. I closed my eyes trying to absorb the sensation.

"Don't close your eyes. Look at me," she ordered as if she were a part of this.

I did as I was told.

"Good. Now, you will be obedient…"

Another strike.

"You will be submissive…"

Another strike.

"And you will do what you are told to do."

Another strike.

"Yes, maam."

"Don't let this have to happen again," she said ending the call.

As soon as she did, Dante leaned over me pressing his clothed body against mine. Feeling his large hard cock pressed against my hip, and the paddle resting on the back of my leg, he whispered in my ear.

"You're gonna be my good boy, aren't you?"

The rumble of his low voice sent shivers through me. I should have been mad at him. He had humiliated me in front of my sister. But all I could do was yearn for his cock in my ass.

"Yes, sir!" I crooned.

"Say it louder."

"Yes, sir! I will be a good boy from now on!"

I could hear his teeth drag across his bottom lip.

"That's my boy," he replied before slapping the back of my thigh with the leather. As my head flipped back in agony, he unbuttoned his pants, pulled out his monster cock, found my hole, and fucked me.

Like with his choice of who to call, he was merciless. Slamming me into the counter as he drilled me, he whispered in my ear.

"You're so beautiful. You're the hottest thing I've ever seen. I want you. I want every bit of you. You're perfect. I could never find anyone better than you."

This was too much. It was all too much. Ripped out of this world, I spiraled into a new one. In it was only me and him. Humiliation, pain, love, they were physical objects that pushed through me. Whipped from one emotion to the next, my achingly hard cock flinched a final time before I screamed and sprayed.

Hearing me, Dante grabbed my hair. Forcing my legs apart, he crouched and really let loose. I was a rag doll in his hands. Pressed onto the counter, I wasn't going anywhere. And when he had worn a man-sized hole in me, and I could no longer hold on, he bellowed and filled me with his juices.

His grip on my hair had been the only thing holding me up. Releasing me and falling into an exhausted stupor, Dante collapsed onto me. No longer held up, I melted onto the counter. Dante's heavy breaths engulfed me. It smelled like his kiss.

Not there long, Dante pushed his hand under my chest wanting to wrap his arms around me. I wanted it too, but I had nothing left in me. I was too fucked to move.

Content to feel him on top of me, I didn't have to settle. As soon as he caught his breath, he stood up, lifted me into his arms, and carried me to his bed. Resting my head onto his shoulder, I watched my cloak drag behind us. Placed onto the mattress, I was quickly disrobed.

Still too fucked to budge, I watched as Dante undressed. His tattooed chest rippled as he moved. His stomach was a washboard.

Lowering his unzipped pants, he next removed his underwear. Although he wasn't hard, his cock was still quite full. It would be the perfect size to suck. That I could fit down my throat. I wouldn't get the opportunity to, though, because once he was naked, he climbed onto the bed beside me and pulled me into his arms.

I don't know why, but it was then that everything that had happened released something within me. As he gently cradled me, I suddenly started to cry. It wasn't me crying, of course. It was Shiro. I felt nothing like that. Usually I felt nothing at all.

But, apparently Shiro was a candy ass. He was everything I wasn't. And as he bawled pathetically, Dante held him tight. With his large hand cupping the back of my head, he buried me into him.

Why was Shiro the only version of me that my father could love? What was it about Kuroi that was so easy to pass around? These were just questions for me, but Shiro blubbered about it. So pathetic. Thank God I was nothing like that. How embarrassing would it be if I was?

Dante continued to hold Shiro until he couldn't cry any more. It was only when his inferno tantrum was done that I could relax. Listening to my husband's powerful heartbeats, I felt safe. And buried in his strong arms, I slowly drifted off to sleep.

****Author note: Wondering what would have happened if Kuroi chose the bare hand emoji? It's shocking! Read the alternate sex scene by becoming a Patron on BookishBoyfriend.com. It's the author's new website* *where you can have steamy chats with characters from the author's sexy romances. Read the alternate sex scene and try out the steamy chat for free. And don't worry, the chats only get NSFW if you want them to.* ☺ *Click here to go there now.*

Chapter 12

Dante

What the fuck had I done? Had I broken Kuroi? The man I had married didn't cry. He barely had emotions at all. It was like he was a different person.

He had called himself Shiro. I had thought he was roleplaying. That's why I went along with it.

And he knew the safe word. I had made sure of it. He could have stopped what I was doing at any time. So, why didn't he? Just when I thought I understood him and could predict his responses, he did this.

Of course, in a hundred years I wouldn't have guessed that I would have made him do what I did last night. But I had. I don't know what came over me.

I was just gonna have him bend over my knee and then paddle him. …Okay, that's not completely true. From the time he requested it, I had decided to come up with something on the fly. And then I remembered Yuki telling me that Kuroi needed a firm hand.

I have to be honest, her telling me that kinda pissed me off. I can't tell you why it did. I went to her for advice. She gave it to me. But it was the way she said it. It was like she was the grand empress, and I knew nothing. She made me feel like I didn't deserve Kuroi or something.

So, with Kuroi standing in front of me looking like he did, it just came to me. And I hadn't considered how Yuki would respond seeing Kuroi dressed like he was, but I definitely wouldn't have predicted that she would've responded how she had.

It was like the two of us were working together. But I couldn't support any of what she was saying about Kuroi knowing his place. Kuroi knew his place. It was by my side being the king he was.

Yet, hearing her say those things, I still went along with it. I was turned on by everything too much to stop. It had to have hurt Kuroi, right? That's why after bringing him to my bed, he collapsed into tears. So, why didn't he use the safe word? Had he forgotten it?

"Morning," Kuroi said to me with a smile.

"Morning," I replied not having slept for a second.

"Am I going to have to handcuff you today?" he asked, looking refreshed and relaxed.

"You don't need handcuffs because I'm never letting you go."

Kuroi stared at me for a second and then leaned forward and kissed me. Relaxing onto the pillow, he stared into my eyes.

"About last night," I began.

"Let's not talk about last night," he said still contently smiling.

But we had to, didn't we? I had never been a chick about these things, but if ever we needed to talk, it would be about what happened last night.

"I just want to make sure. You remembered our safe word, right?"

Kuroi's smile widened amused. Reaching over and placing his hand on my cheek, he reassured me.

"Yes, I remember our safe word."

"Just checking," I said, not feeling better about things, but knowing I hadn't crossed a line.

Reassured, the muscles in my shoulders unclenched. My whole body did. With it came the wave of exhaustion from being awake all night. It dragged my eyes closed. And just as I was going to let myself fall asleep, Kuroi said,

"Oh, I never got a chance to tell you why I had deserved a treat last night."

"You didn't," I said without the strength to reopen my eyes.

"I found your uncle."

"I figured. Where is he?"

"Tied up in a warehouse in the Bronx."

My eyes snapped open.

"What?"

"I figured you'd want to talk to him and I thought I'd make it easy for you," Kuroi said pleased with himself.

"That's… I don't…" I muttered fighting for words. "Why would you do that?"

"Because he might be here to kill you. He can't kill you if he's tied up in a warehouse."

"He's been there all night?" I said fully awake and sitting up.

"I didn't mean to leave him there. I got distracted by something. What was it again? That's right, your cock up my ass," he said amused.

Sprinting out of bed to get ready, I told Kuroi, "You have to take me to him."

Rolling over to watch me, he replied, "He's been there all night. If he needed to pee, he's peed himself by now. What's another hour in bed?"

"This isn't a joke, Kuroi. You need to take me to him now."

"You're no fun," my husband said reluctantly complying.

Dressed, I didn't let Kuroi go through his usual routine of choosing an outfit and putting on makeup. Still, he managed to look stylish and hot as hell. Matteo thought of himself as some type of pretty boy. But it was

Kuroi who always looked like he stepped off of a runway.

"What are you waiting for? Let's go," he told me entering the living room as if he was the one waiting on me.

Hopping into my car, we drove out of the city and into the Bronx.

"My father has warehouses in every borough," he explained.

"To store his product?"

"They are more like distribution hubs. He has a few and rotates between them before selling them. This one's empty."

That told me a lot about Sato's organization. If we ever did go to war, I now knew how to cripple him. I wasn't sure if Kuroi had meant to tell me what he had, but there was no way I would use the information in a way that could hurt him.

Approaching the warehouse, I understood how Sato could use it for distribution. The only way in was through an alley. And behind a fence and small patio, the place was very easy to secure.

"What did you tell him when you grabbed him?"

"Does it look like I have henchmen? I didn't grab him. I convinced him to follow me."

"How did you do that?"

"Turns out that you and your uncle share a taste in men. All I had to do was look at him and he started following me."

"Did you fuck him?" I said my temper racing to a boil.

"What are you crazy?"

"How am I supposed to know what you meant by that?"

"You're supposed to know that I'm not going to fuck your uncle, the man who might be here to kill you."

"Good that you know that."

"What the fuck, Dante? I did something nice for you."

I calmed myself.

"You're right. What you did was good. I just… I just can't think about you with anyone else. I swear to God, if anything Yuki told me about what happened to you as a kid had been true, I would murder everyone who ever laid a hand on you."

Kuroi stared at me, frozen.

"Why are you looking at me like that?"

"What did Yuki tell you about my childhood?"

"She didn't tell me anything about your childhood. What she told me was some fucked up story about you being some sort of Japanese apprentice or some shit."

"A kagema," Kuroi said lowering his eyes. "And you didn't believe her?"

"Come on, there was no way she was serious about that. I mean, Sato's an asshole, but you're his son."

Kuroi eyes met the floor as he looked away.

I was driving but the sight of him captured my full attention.

"Wait, does that have to do with why you were crying last night?"

"I said I don't want to talk about what happened last night."

I could feel myself preparing to explode. I had to pull over.

"It's right up there," Kuroi said pointing.

"I don't give a fuck where it is." With the car off, I turned in my seat to face him. "Look, I'm sorry about what I did last night. The truth is that after our first few nights together, I went to your sister to get advice on how to handle you."

"How to handle me? What am I, a dog?"

"No! Have you forgotten what you did to me? You fuckin' stabbed me the night you moved in. The next night you threw a fuckin' casserole dish at me. Even with my ability to heal when I shifted, Lorenzo had to stitch me up. I almost bled to death goin' to him. So, yeah, I needed help on how to handle you so I didn't end up dead."

That shut Kuroi up.

Feeling like I was too enthusiastic in making my point, I took his hand.

"That wasn't the point I was trying to make. I went to Yuki because she knew you better than I did. But, what she told me, it was beyond belief. She said that Sato had made you…"

"Kagema," he said still unable to look at me.

"That's it. And she said that Sato, gave you to someone as, like, a rent boy?"

"Rent boy? No, it's different than that," Kuroi replied.

"It shouldn't be anywhere close to that. Tell me this is one of your fucked up fantasies. Or, tell me anything. But, if you tell me it's true…"

"It's true," he said meeting my gaze.

Fire exploded within me as my wolf fought to get out. I was a cauldron ready to boil over. I would kill every man who had touched him. Then I would kill Sato. I would cut off his fingers one by one and feed it to him.

"Take me to him," I demanded.

"Who? Your uncle?"

"Fuck my uncle. The man Sato gave you to."

"He's dead."

I struggled to catch my breath.

"Then take me to the next one."

"He's dead too. They're all dead."

"You killed them? You should have."

"I don't remember doing it. I don't remember killing any of them."

"What do you mean you don't remember?"

"They died of heart attacks. All of them. I'm poison."

The pain in Kuroi's voice pulled me back.

"What are you talking about?"

"I'm the poison that killed them. Anyone who sleeps with me dies. You're going to die."

"How am I gonna die?"

"I don't know," he said melting into regret.

I took Kuroi's hand.

"Listen to me, Kuroi. You're not gonna hurt me."

"You don't know that."

"I do. You aren't poison. You're everything I've dreamed of. I'll do everything to protect you and you'll do everything to protect me."

"What if I can't protect you from myself?"

"I don't want you to protect me from who you are. I want everything you have. I want it all. You can't scare me away. I'm here and I'm your husband. And the way I know I'll be around forever is because I know you'll make sure of it. You can count on me having your back and I know I can count on you having mine."

Kuroi didn't respond. He didn't have to. I knew what I had said was true and there was nothing he could say to convince me otherwise.

But as much as I had calmed down, I was still enraged. Sato was going to die for what he had done to Kuroi. I was going to rip his head from his neck with my bare hands. I would do the same to anyone who stood in my way. But first,

"Where's my uncle?"

"That's the door there," he said pointing to the fence and warehouse door.

"Show me," I told him before we got out of the car, and he led the way.

Opening the warehouse's door, it was completely empty except for one thing. At the very center of it was a chair. On it was a man I didn't recognize. Hearing the door open, his head popped up and he groaned. Not only was he tied to the chair and gagged, he was blindfolded.

I looked at Kuroi who met my eyes blankly. I gestured for him to get a glass of water. He thought for a second and then exited the building. Before I reached the chair, Kuroi was back with a cup. Falling into my wake, I approached the chair and stared down at the man.

Although I had never seen him before, he looked like a Ricci. He looked more like Lorenzo than either Matteo or me. But the family resemblance was clear.

Feeling me in front of him, his muffled groans turned into garbled speech.

"I'm gonna remove the gag from your mouth. Are you gonna make me regret it?"

He calmed and then shook his head, 'no.'

Slowly reaching down, I loosened his gag and removed it.

"Gratsi. Gratsi. Thank you," he said in an Italian accent.

"Now, I have some water for you. But first you're gonna need to answer a few of my questions. Do you understand me?"

"I understand. Yes."

"And you're gonna be honest with me?"

"I'll tell you the truth. Whatever you need me to say."

I looked back at Kuroi who held the cup expressionless.

"What's your name?"

"I'm nobody. I'm just here visiting family. You have the wrong guy."

"Are you Vincent Ricci?"

He froze hearing the name.

"I said, is your name Vincent Ricci?"

"I don't know what you would want with me. I never hurt nobody. I'm just here visiting family."

I took that as a yes.

"Are you here to do a job?"

"I'm not here for nothin'. I told you. I'm just here visiting family."

Stepping closer to him, I balled my fist and clocked him as hard as I could on his jaw. The old man rocked into silence. I had to be careful how I did this. I was still raging from what Kuroi had told me. And I had nearly knocked him out.

I tapped the other side of his face to wake him.

"I told you. You gotta be honest with me. Are you going to be honest with me?"

"Si. Si, I'll be honest."

"Now, were you allowed back into the country in exchange for doing a job?"

"Si. My brother needed me to do a job."

"Your brother said you could come back in the country if you took care of his son. Is that right? Dante Ricci?"

He again froze, this time trying to figure out who I was.

"That's what he wanted me to do. But I wasn't going to do it."

"What were gonna do, then? Were you gonna warn him?"

"Yes, I was gonna warn him."

"You were gonna find him and let him know that his father had sent you to kill him?"

"I could never hurt him. He's my nephew."

"So, what were you gonna do instead? Were you gonna offer to help him kill his father?"

He froze, this time confused.

"No. I wasn't going to do that?"

"Then what were you gonna do, huh?"

"Who are you? Dante? Matteo? Are you Matteo?"

I glanced back at Kuroi.

"Yeah I'm Matteo. And you were gonna betray Pa, weren't you? After he let you come back, you were gonna tell my bitch ass of a brother why you were here, weren't you?" I said building to a shout.

"I swear, I wasn't going to."

"Then why haven't you completed the job?"

"You were supposed to give me the gun. I was where I was told to be. You didn't show up. I waited for an hour. I thought you weren't coming. If you give me the gun, I'll do the job."

"And you could do this to family?" I said feeling the anger pulse through me.

"Your father told me that fag is fucking the son of his enemy. That's not family. Family doesn't do that. He's a disgrace. A disgrace!" he yelled. "Give me the gun and I'll take care of him like your father asked. Untie me and give me the gun," he said with a mixture of anger and fear.

I looked back at Kuroi a final time. His eyes reflected what I felt. I knew what I would do next. And as my wolf clawed through to the surface, my bones broke welcoming him.

Staring out through its eyes, I saw the way my wolf looked at Kuroi. He desired Kuroi as much as I did. But, turning back to my uncle, my wolf growled and then did what it had come to do.

Perhaps I should have been nervous driving to Sunday dinner at my parent's house. After all, my father had sent his brother to kill me. I wasn't though. It didn't even matter that this would be the first time my father met my new husband.

I didn't know how father would react to him. Dressed as Kuroi was, I couldn't imagine it going over well. He was wearing a jumpsuit sort of thing that was like what he wore to dinner with Matteo. It wasn't the same one though because this one was dark blue without the fancy stitching. And this one had sleeves.

He also didn't wear much makeup. At least it didn't look like he did. It took him forever to get dressed so maybe he was going for an invisible look, or whatever you call it. Either way, I could barely stop myself from peeking over at my husband as we drove.

"Did I tell you that you look beautiful?" I said reaching across the car to take his hand.

"You haven't," he said with a smirk.

"You look beautiful," I said pulling his hand to my lips and kissing it.

"Thank you," he said with a smile. "I'm nervous."

I looked at him doubtfully. "Why would you be nervous?"

"I want your mother to like me."

"Don't worry. She will."

"Does she know about me?"

"Everyone knows about you. Everyone knows I married you."

"But, I mean, does she know about you and me?" he asked squeezing my hand.

He was asking if she knew that I was falling in love with the man I married. For that to be true, she would have had to know that I liked men.

"She doesn't know how I feel about you," I admitted.

"And how's that?"

"What? Are you gonna make me say it?"

"I'm not going to make you do anything," he said looking away.

I didn't want him to think that I was anything other than head over heels for him. I didn't know it was possible to be as happy as I was with Kuroi. I felt awake and alive when I was with him. Being with Kuroi gave my life purpose.

I was put on this earth to protect him. It wasn't like he needed much protection. He could take care of himself. But in spite of how deadly he was, he seemed to have no defense when it came to his family.

I didn't like what Yuki had said to him during that Facetime. It's weird, though. Ever since then, he's been walking around with less weight on his shoulders. I can't explain it. But if I had to do it over again, I wouldn't do it.

Then there was Sato. Kuroi has since told me how many times Sato had given Kuroi to someone in exchange for a better deal. It was three times. I was the fourth.

The first time Kuroi was a child. He had no choice. The next two times, Kuroi wasn't as young. He could have refused. He was definitely old enough to refuse to marry me. But he hadn't. He went through with it without fighting back.

Perhaps it was his demon's power, but Sato had some sort of hold on him. What else would he do if Sato asked him to? Could he refuse his father's wishes even if he wanted to?

My new purpose in life was to protect him from that. Sato would die for what he did to him.

"I love you," I said staring through the windshield with my hand engulfing his.

When he didn't say it back, I glanced over at him. He looked conflicted. That was fine. My loving him didn't require him saying it back.

"I will always be there for you. Do you hear me? From now on, you come first. You are my family and my pack. I want you to know that."

I relaxed into my seat having told him. It was enough that he knew it. Finding a spot on my parents' street, I pulled over and parked.

"Are you ready for this?" I asked Kuroi squeezing his hand one last time.

"If you are," he replied squeezing my hand back.

Getting out of the car, I waited for Kuroi to retrieve our contribution to dinner from the trunk. With it in hand, I led him to the steps of the brownstone I grew up in and ascended.

Knocking and entering, the first person I saw was Lorenzo.

"You're late," he told me clearly on his second glass of bourbon.

"You can't rush perfection," I told him raising my eyebrows hinting at my own frustration.

"I didn't want to be here," Lorenzo reminded me.

"I know. Thank you for coming. It is a momentous occasion for our family and it was important that you be here for it."

I grabbed Lorenzo by the back of the neck, stared into his eyes, and kissed him on the cheek.

"Thank you," I told him letting him go.

When Kuroi entered behind me holding the box, Lorenzo greeted him with a nod. Kuroi coolly nodded back. I followed Kuroi's shifted gaze and found Matteo staring him down.

There was still tension between the two and I had to take my husband's side on whatever was going on. But Matteo had made his loyalty clear by not showing up to give Uncle Vinny the gun.

"Matteo," I said grabbing him by the neck pulling him to me. "I want you to crush whatever beef you have with Kuroi. Do you hear me? He's my husband. You're my brother. Don't make me have to choose. Because he's family too."

"I hear you," Matteo said before I kissed him and let him go.

Watching him as he approached Kuroi, I stood ready to react.

"Kuroi," Matteo said approaching him.

"Matteo," Kuroi said staring at him as if my brother was a snake about to attack.

"Do you want me to take that?" Matteo offered referring to Kuroi's box.

"He has it," I interjected wanting to present it personally.

After Matteo, I introduced Kuroi to Giovanni and Marco and then stepped into the kitchen to find Ma. Wearing her white and blue apron with the bird print on it, I watched her as she dished up the serving plates. Without turning around she said,

"I hear you're responsible for Lorenzo joining us today?"

"I asked him to be here. Ma, can I introduce you to someone?"

She turned around spotting Kuroi in the doorway behind me. She stared at him.

"I want you to meet my husband, Kuroi."

Her eyes bounced to me. She didn't know what to say. I had to add some context.

"It was an arranged marriage to link our two packs after what Matteo did…" I caught myself. Ma was in the dark about what we got up to in pack business. So she definitely didn't need to hear about what Matteo had done. "But it doesn't matter. Kuroi's my husband now," I said pulling him to me and putting my arm around him. "And I'm happy."

That was when Ma smiled and approached him. Throwing her arms in the air in celebration, she tried to hug Kuroi and was prevented by the box.

"What's this," Ma said asking about the box.

"It's a surprise, Ma."

"Well, do you want to help him with that?" Ma said trying to free Kuroi from the box.

"I got it," I said taking it from him. When I did, Ma hugged him.

"It's always a blessing to have another son."

She turned to me. "Don't think this relieves you of your duty to give me a grandchild."

Kuroi's eyes darted to me.

"One step at a time, Ma."

"Yes, one step," she agreed. "Sit, sit. Your father will be down soon. I'll set another plate."

With everyone gathering in the dining room, I took my seat at the opposite end of the table and placed the box on the side table behind me. When we were all settled, Pa descended the stairs like an emperor. I couldn't tell whether he was surprised or disappointed to see me. Either way, I stared at him coldly.

His eyes momentarily turned to Kuroi before looking away. Pa didn't like Kuroi. Considering who his father is, I didn't know if Pa ever would.

That was okay. He didn't have to like Kuroi. But he sure as hell was going to respect him as the man married to the alpha.

Pa sat without a word and Ma finished setting the food on the table. After she sat and before she led grace, I stood.

"If no one minds I want to say something before we start because we have a special guest here today."

Everyone turned to look at Kuroi.

"I know only a few of you have met him. The rest of you have heard about him. But we can all thank Pa for him being here today. That's right. It was Pa who invited him."

Everyone turned to Pa.

"I never invited your disgrace into my home," he sniped.

I turned to him.

"First of all, you better watch your fucking mouth before I cut out your tongue."

"Dante!" Ma said shocked.

"Dante, you can't talk to Pa like that," Matteo chimed in.

"I can't talk to Pa like that, huh? You think you can talk to me like that? You wanna see what happens if you keep talkin'?" I said readying to shift.

Matteo backed down. I continued.

"You all might be thinking that I'm referring to Kuroi. Although it is a special occasion to have my husband here with the family for the first time, I'm not. Who I'm referring to is…"

I turned behind me and retrieved the box. Forcing it onto the table in front of me, I untied the bow holding it together and lifted the top off.

"…it's Uncle Vinny."

Pa looked into the eyes of his brother's head and gasped. He flung himself back in his chair in shock. Everyone did, except Kuroi. My husband, instead, stuck a roll into his mouth, which was a bit of a taboo because at this table, we didn't eat until after we prayed. But he was new here, so I didn't correct him.

"What the fuck, Dante?" Lorenzo said after scrabbling away from the table.

"Oh, don't thank me for Uncle Vinny being here. You have to thank Pa. Isn't that right? Because after years of banishment, Pa offered our Uncle Vinny a deal. He could come back as long as he did one thing for Pa, kill me."

Everyone gasped.

"Don't fake your fuckin' surprise, Matteo. I know you were in on it."

"I swear to you, Dante, I could never go through with it. I could never betray you like that!" He proclaimed now fearing for his life.

"I don't know if that's true. But you didn't and that's what's important. That's why your head isn't in the box next to his. Do you understand me, Matteo?"

When he didn't respond, I repeated it louder.

"I said, do you understand?"

"Yeah, Dante. I understand."

"Good."

I turned to Pa and circled the table to where he still sat, his eyes darting between his brother's head and me.

"Now the question is, what do I do with Pa? You hired someone to kill me. A family member, no less. And why? Because I married someone who will probably end up being the love of my life."

I got close and looked him in the eyes.

"Ya know, if you can't accept that, I should probably put you out of your misery now. Because neither he nor I are going anywhere. Would you prefer that, Pa? You want me to put you out of your misery?"

Pa's mouth moved without words coming out. I could see that he wanted to shift but he didn't dare.

"What was that? You need to speak up a little louder. Everyone here needs to hear what you say."

"I can accept it," he said practically shitting himself.

"And you're not just saying that, right? Because I remember what you taught us about how to handle liars."

"I'm tellin' you the truth," he said still in shock.

I dipped my chin in satisfaction.

"Good. Good. Then that's settled. Come on everyone, take your seats. Let's enjoy Ma's delicious Sunday dinner."

Everyone stared at me not moving. Once I sat down, Lorenzo said,

"Dante, you can't expect us to eat with that thing there," he said gesturing to the head.

"Lorenzo, that is your Uncle Vinny. Sit fuckin' down and have some fuckin' respect!" I said slowly losing my cool.

"Dante, Ma," Matteo said gesturing to our mother who was as white as a ghost.

"I wasn't the one who invited him here. If you have a problem with this, tell it to Pa. Now everybody, sit your fuckin' asses down and eat!"

When everyone was again seated, I led the family in grace. I didn't say anything clever or witty. I just got the job done and dished up.

"The roast is very good, Ma. You've outdone yourself," I told her.

"Yes, my compliments to the chef," Kuroi added with a smile.

It didn't end up being the most relaxed dinner our family had ever had, but it was also not the least. How relaxed our dinners were was always a matter of perspective. Growing up, there were times when Pa would whip us so hard the skin would peel from our flesh. When dinner followed, Pa would make us sit and eat as relaxed as could be.

Today, the shoe was on the other foot. Pa ate Ma's roast unable to take his eyes off what could have been his fate. I, on the other hand, had assured Kuroi's and my survival, at least at the hands of my pack.

The only thing left to do after this had to do with Sato. I wasn't sure I could just kill him. He was one of the most protected men in New York City. Getting to him might take some time. Taking the head with us when we left, I put our three heads together to come up with a plan.

I'm joking, of course. We got rid of Uncle Vinny's head like we did his body, with the help of Sato's facilities. I did have to hand it to Sato, the Yakuza was an organized bunch. I could learn a thing or two from them. It was no wonder Sato was able to capture the heroin trade in New York so quickly.

In some ways, I admired him. That didn't change what I was going to do to him. He had earned his place in hell the minute he sold Kuroi into sex slavery. And I wasn't going to deny him his rewards.

The only question was, how would I do it? And how would Kuroi respond if I told him?

243

Chapter 13

Kuroi

I was shaken driving home from dinner with Dante's family. I couldn't believe it. How did Dante's mother make the roast taste that good? I have eaten at the best restaurants around the world. None of them could compare to what his mother made.

I never knew my mother. As far as I could tell, she was dead. Why else would my father take me in?

And I've never met Yuki's mother. I've seen her at a distance. But when my father was assigned to New York, I went with him and a chef prepared all of our meals.

Sitting around the Ricci table, I couldn't help but wonder about what it would have been like to grow up in a family like Dante's. Having a mother who slaved over the stove cooking for her family and siblings who gathered on Sunday to enjoy it.

The severed head part, I was familiar with. You can only be around my father for so long without seeing a severed head. But the other stuff. Yeah, there was tension between Dante and his brothers but they all clearly loved each other.

In spite of being ordered by his father, Matteo refused to betray Dante. He defied his father for his brother. I couldn't imagine what that type of love felt like. The closest I've experienced was when Dante's uncle said that thing about Dante and me and Dante's hot wolf killed him for it.

Besides Yuki, no one has ever cared about me. I grew up desperate for someone to acknowledge me. But my father never even looked at me.

Eventually I figured out how to make him look. I made it so he couldn't ignore me. I demanded his attention, and he responded by selling me.

If it wasn't for Yuki, I might have lost my mind growing up like I did. Without her I wouldn't have known what love was. She was the only one who ever loved me. And I killed anyone else who tried.

"What's the matter?" Dante asked as we pulled into his parking spot.

"What do you mean?" I asked.

"You're crying."

"Don't be ridiculous," I said offended.

"You are," he insisted before reaching across the car and wiping his finger against my cheek. Showing it to me, his finger was wet.

Startled, I quickly wiped my face and escaped the car.

"I wasn't crying."

Joining me as we walked to the elevator, Dante stared at me concerned.

"Did what happen freak you out?"

"What?"

"The head thing and dinner."

I looked at him and laughed.

"You're dumb but you're cute."

He stopped.

"Look, Kuroi, I love you. I've told you that I love you. And I will do anything to protect you. But you gotta meet me halfway. You can't just break out crying and not tell me what's going on. How do you think that makes me feel?"

I stopped and looked back frustrated.

"I said I wasn't crying."

"Then what was it, allergies?" he asked sarcastically. "Was robot fluid leaking from your face? I hate to tell you this but you're not a robot. You feel things even if you can't admit that you do."

"Listen to me, Dante, I wasn't crying!" I insisted.

"And what about the other night?"

I froze.

"What other night?"

"The night when… we did that thing and you… you know… lost it?"

"That wasn't me."

"Well, I sure hope it was you. We just got married. It's too soon to be inviting another man into our bed," he joked.

"Dante," I said overwhelmed.

He grabbed me by the shoulders and stared down into my eyes.

"You don't have to do this. I know I'm not that great at communicating. I mean, why the fuck would I be. But I know it's important so I'm trying here. If I hurt you, you gotta tell me. That's what the safe word is for, right? So I don't hurt you. You can't let me keep doing things that hurt you."

"You haven't done anything to hurt me," I insisted.

"Then why were you crying?"

"Because my life is fucked up, Dante. I don't know if you know this about me, but everyone calls me the spider demon. And they deserve to."

"No one deserves to talk to you like that."

"Yes they do. Because I am the spider demon. I will kill you, Dante. I don't want to. And I won't even know I'm doing it. But one day I'm going to wake up and find you lying next to me dead. I can't take that, Dante. I don't want to lose you. I can't lose you. I love you."

"Wait, you love me?"

"Yeah… Or, I don't know. How the fuck is someone like me supposed to know what love is?"

I fell into Dante's arms and yes, I cried. It wasn't Shiro, it was Kuroi. Or, maybe it wasn't. I didn't know who the fuck I was anymore.

"I don't want to kill you, Dante."

"Listen to me. You're not gonna kill me."

"I am. I'm going to kill you and then I'm going to kill myself right after. Because I don't want to live without you."

"Kuroi, you're not gonna kill me. I know you. You hear me. I know who you are and you would never hurt me."

"I'm sorry, Dante," I said through my tears.

"You have nothing to be sorry about. You can never hurt me."

"You mean, again?"

Dante laughed.

"That's right. You could never hurt me, again. You got me pretty good when you stabbed me. And it took a couple of shifts to heal what you did to my skull. But we know each other now. And the man I know as Kuroi, will never hurt me… again."

I laughed and sniffed. Pulling away from him, I wiped the tears from my eyes. Looking down at Dante's shirt, it was covered in makeup.

"If I'm not going to kill you, I'm going to have to invest in waterproof makeup."

Dante looked down at his foundation-smeared white shirt.

"How the fuck were you wearing makeup? I swear to god that you weren't wearing any when we left this morning."

I looked up at Dante and shook my head.

"It's a good thing you're cute."

Collecting myself, we continued to the elevator and headed up to our apartment. When the elevator doors to our place opened, my body reacted. Placing my hand on him, I stopped Dante.

"What?" he whispered seeing me readying for a fight.

I gestured for him to stay where he was. Replying with a look that said that there was no way he was just going to stand there, I gestured emphatically, and he obeyed.

Leaning out of the elevator and finding no one behind the door, I got low and eased out. I knew that scent. It was faint and I wasn't sure who it was. But I was sure that it shouldn't have been here.

Scanning the open space I found no one. That didn't tell me anything. There were at least three rooms I couldn't see into and…

"Yuki," I said suddenly realizing who it was.

Moments after saying it, my sister walked out of Dante's bedroom. She wasn't dressed as she usually was in her stylish Japanese inspired garb. She was in all black as if trying to blend into the night.

"Yuki?" Dante asked leaving the elevator and seeing her. "What are you doing here?"

"Visiting my brother," she said as calmly as ever.

Dante looked at my sister and then at me. He wasn't buying it. Neither was I.

"Can you lock the door?" I asked Dante.

I didn't actually know if he could. I knew it required a key to get to our floor. But that didn't mean he could stop someone from getting out.

"I can lock it," he said sticking a key into the elevator panel.

"That's not necessary," Yuki said casually.

"Neither is coming here when I'm not," I pointed out.

Yuki relaxed and headed to the couch.

"Are you not going to offer your sister something to drink?"

I didn't know what she was doing but I decided to play along.

"Of course. Where are my manors?"

"They are deplorable," Yuki proclaimed.

I wasn't sure if she was joking or not. Knowing her, she wasn't.

"Tea?" I asked her.

"If it's what you have," she said disapprovingly.

"It is," I confirmed before heading to the kitchen to prepare it.

"Wait, are we just going to pretend that it isn't as weird as fuck that she was in our place when we got here?"

Yuki responded before I could.

"Considering the facetime I received from Shiro, I thought we had progressed past weird."

That shut Dante up for a second.

"Listen, having him call you was a mistake."

"Perhaps this is my mistake. How many are each of us allowed?"

Again, Dante was quiet. Having no response, he clenched his jaw and headed to his room leaving my sister and me alone.

"We only have tea bags," I informed Yuki.

I didn't have to see her to know that she was displeased. Selecting the only one from Dante's stock that was worth drinking, I added water to the coffee pot and brought it to a boil. Not saying a word the entire time, I collected a mug from the cupboard and poured us cups.

Yuki didn't wait to make her feelings clear. Putting it down as soon as she received it, she stared daring me to defy my upbringing by drinking tea from a mug. I got it all the way to my lips before putting it down. I could try to fight it but like my father, Yuki's cold stare had a power over me. As little as I could defy my father's wishes, I could defy Yuki even less.

"So, why are you here?" I asked having waited long enough.

Straightening her back, she said, "To bring you home."

"I am home," I told her confused.

"No. You are where father put you."

I couldn't deny that. Father declared I would marry Dante and that was why I was here.

"That might have been how it started, but Dante is my husband now. I am where I am supposed to be."

"Where you are supposed to be is home."

"That's what I'm trying to tell you, Yuki. I am home."

"Were you home when Father gave you away the first time?"

"No," I said repulsed by the thought.

"But, at the time you thought you were home."

I opened my mouth to deny it and then stopped remembering what had happened. It wasn't the first year with my father's business partner that Yuki was referring to. It was during the second. Or, perhaps it was the third. But, after a while, I had stopped fighting my circumstances and had given in to them.

Past what went on at night, I had had freedom. I couldn't go anywhere without his permission or have friends. But as long as I was accompanied by one of his men, I could do whatever I wanted. I could drink. I could blow off my tutor. Hell, I could blow my tutor if I wanted.

In that hazy delusion, I began to see myself as royalty. Think about it. I was caged, my body wasn't my own, but I could buy anything I wanted, and treat people however I pleased. I was a Disney princess.

"I was young and stupid back then. Now I am not."

"But again, you think you are home. The new cage father has put you in is again your home. Would you have left your first home if someone hadn't freed you?"

"Freed me? I freed myself," I said knowing my master had been the spider demon's first victim.

"And the second man father gave you to?"

"Then too," I said less confidently.

"And the third?"

"Yes," I said rattled by Yuki's questions.

"Hm," she chirped before grabbing the mug and taking a sip.

Chills crawled up my arms. My heart raced as I fought to look calm. She knew something and she wanted me to know that she did. But what? Did she know how I had killed them? How could she know that?

"I'm not leaving here," I told her.

"You will," she said confidently.

"I'm not going to do what I did before?"

"What did you do? Tell me, how did you free yourself?"

"I… killed them," I admitted as a feeble attempt at a threat.

"Who have you killed? Tell me. Who do you have the strength to kill?"

I didn't need to tell her. Everyone knew what they called me. I killed my lovers. Even the ones I liked. She knew this. Why was she making me say it?

And then it hit me. She was making me say it because… I hadn't. What hadn't I done?

I had killed them. They were all dead. I woke up next to all of them. Each was dead.

I got up overwhelmed by the memory. Why was she making me relive this? Each time I fell asleep next to them and woke to a cold corpse and the smell of shit or piss where their bowels had relaxed and relieved itself.

I paced the room remembering the stench and horror of it all. I remembered my tears and the way I screamed when I realized that I had done it again. I remembered the call to my father, sobbing uncontrollably. I remembered the shame as my father's men carried the bodies away.

I was the spider demon. I killed everyone who dared love me. And I remembered one other thing. Maybe not the first time it happened or even the second, but the other times I remembered there being a scent in the room the night before they died.

It was faint. It was always faint. It was more of an instinct than anything else. A registration that lingered just below my consciousness. It was the same scent I smelled… tonight.

"You!" I said, it hitting me like a sledgehammer. "It was never me. It was you!"

She stared at me unfazed, unyielding.

"But, how? Why?"

"You are mine," Yuki said casually. "Father gave you to me."

"I… What?"

"You will come home because father gave you to me and you belong home."

"Like… your doll?"

My mind spiraled trying to understand everything she was saying. Had she killed all of my lovers out of jealousy? Or, was it possession? Did she believe that she owned me? That no one else was allowed to have me?

I stared at Yuki, who stared back unflinching and calm. She believed this. She thought that I belonged to her. And when father gave me away…

"You aren't possessed by a house spirit. You are Yuki-Anno, the Snow Woman cursed to wonder the cold alone. You kill out of vengeance."

She stared at me coldly as a chill surrounded us. And then it hit me.

"It was you who whispered in his ear," I said remembering what the customs officer said about her brother.

She had said that there was someone who put the idea into his head that the Italian girl was into that stuff. It would have had to have been someone who had access to him and who he would trust.

The brother had worked directly with my father. That meant that he was frequently at the compound. And if Yuki told him something, he would at least consider it.

"Why would you tell that man something like that? Couldn't you see where it would lead?"

Yuki blinked. It was slow and icy. It told me everything.

"You did know. This was your plan. You wanted war. But why?"

Her still demeanor couldn't mask the feral scream with which she thought it. Unable to contain herself for a second longer, she told me.

"If he can take away something that's mine, then I can take away something that's his."

I fell back into the couch stunned. For so long I had thought I was a monster. No, I had thought I was worse than a monster because monsters didn't kill what they loved.

The worst part was that I could never remember doing any of it. That meant that I could never be trusted.

I could never allow myself to love anything, and I couldn't trust myself if I did.

But now I understood. It was the one person who I thought loved me that I couldn't trust. I was never really a person to her. I was always just her doll. Her possession. And when her father took it away from her, she plotted to take down his organization as revenge.

"How could you?" I asked allowing the tears to roll down my cheeks. "I thought you loved me."

She said nothing. Her silence ripped my heart from my chest. I was nothing to anyone. No one had ever cared about me, and no one ever would.

It was then that Dante burst out of the bedroom. Like a bull he charged toward Yuki. Seeing him coming, she attempted to back away but couldn't avoid his grasp. His large hand encircled her delicate neck and squeezed. I could see the wolf in him fighting to get out.

"Dante!" I yelled.

"What's this?" he bellowed holding his toothbrush in front of her.

Terror washed across Yuki's face as her gaze locked on the toothbrush.

"What is it?" he shouted.

"What's going on?" I replied panicked.

"There's something on it."

"What is it?"

"I don't know. But she does."

"I don't know anything about it," Yuki protested fighting Dante's hand around her neck while never taking her eyes off the toothbrush.

"You don't, huh? Then I guess it's nothing. Come here," Dante said pushing her back onto the couch and sliding his hand from her neck to her jaw.

Yuki hit and scratched Dante fighting for her life. He barely resisted. Instead, he focused on pinching her mouth open.

"Ahhh!" she screamed.

Dante was relentless. With her lips parted, he pushed his toothbrush into her mouth. She raked her head pleading for him to stop. He wouldn't. And with fiery determination, he brushed her tongue and teeth.

When he was done, he pulled it out. Loosening his grip on her jaw, Yuki cried. I had never seen her express so much emotion. It broke my heart.

"No, no!" she declared no longer fighting Dante's grip.

"What'd you do?" I asked Dante.

"Only she knows," he replied backing off and watching her squirm in anguish.

"Yuki, what did you do?" I yelled at her.

"No, no!" She continued rolling from side to side on the couch.

"I don't understand, Dante. What's going on?"

"I knew there was a reason she was here so I went looking for it," he began as we watched her mourn.

"There was something on my toothbrush. It was like a gel and it didn't have a scent. That's when I remembered what else happened during our wedding. Yuki gave me a drink."

I looked at Dante shocked remembering it.

"But I drank it too."

"No, you drank your own and Yuki controlled who got what."

"She poisoned you."

"And made it look like a heart attack."

As we spoke, Yuki's body convulsed.

"I think, what she put in my drink, she put on my toothbrush. I don't think you were the one to kill those people. I think she was. No one shares a toothbrush."

Yuki, between convulsions, rolled off of the couch and struggled to her knees. I had sympathy for her. I knew I shouldn't. But she was my sister. She had been the only one I loved. She was the only one who had loved me.

"Is there an antidote?" I asked her.

Her eyes bounced up to me. She was possessed with rage. I was finally seeing the real Yuki. Her polite façade was gone. Only the Snow Woman remained.

This was the vengeful demon she had hidden for so long. I hadn't known my sister at all. My entire life had been a lie.

Fighting her way to her feet, she stumbled around looking for nothing in particular. If she had something to counteract her poison, she would have taken it. If there was anything that would have helped, she would have asked for it.

Instead, she haunted the space like a broken ghost. Her skin turned pale completing her transformation. She now looked like the Yuki-Anno she had always been.

Snarling and shaking, she slithered to Dante and me and launched herself at us. I didn't know what she wanted. Perhaps it was nothing. But staring into Dante's eyes with a look that was colder than hell, she whipped her head back, slid down his body and died at our feet.

She had a heart attack. I could tell from the frozen look on her face. I had seen it many times before. It was the look I had woken up to more times than I wanted to remember.

"She had come here to kill you," I said aloud trying to make sense of it all.

"Yeah, she had."

"She wanted me to come home."

"You are home," Dante said wrapping his arms around me pulling me tight.

As the tears again rolled down my face, I leaned into my husband's muscular body. He was built like an oak tree, sturdy, solid, and strong. He was reliable and unyielding. The best thing that had ever happened to me was marrying him. And wherever our life together took us, I would follow.

Unlike anyone, he would protect me. He would hold me when I cried and in his arms I would finally sleep.

"Are you alright?" He asked me looking down at me caringly.

Looking up into his tender eyes, the only thing I could think to say was, "Cherries."

Epilogue

Dante

It wasn't a panic attack. I knew it wasn't. I mean, I had my doubts for a while there when nothing else made sense. But the one thing I had never doubted was Kuroi's innocence.

Having reached his limits, I put Kuroi to bed and disposed of his sister's body. Kuroi didn't want to know what I did with it. She had been betraying him his entire life. He needed time to deal with that. And, what my baby wanted, I was gonna give him.

Storing Yuki's body instead of burning it like we had Uncle Vinny, I removed all traces that she had been at our place including making sure she hadn't bribed the lobby attendant to get in.

She hadn't. It was a mystery how she had gotten in undetected. I didn't like that considering others could probably do the same.

The other thing I did that night was save my toothbrush. I needed to know what it was that she had tried to kill me with.

"Wolfsbane," I told Kuroi days later when my people finished their analysis.

"Wolfsbane is from a flower. She had a garden at the compound. She was always out there taking care of it."

"Its poison works within minutes and the symptoms can be mistaken for a heart attack. I guess she didn't account for my wolf when she put it in my wedding drink. But the stuff is lethal. Only an alpha could have survived.

What makes wolfsbane the perfect poison is that the small amount needed to kill someone usually goes undetected during an autopsy. But the amount they found on my toothbrush was enough to kill a pack."

"That's why she didn't try to save herself," Kuroi concluded. "She knew she couldn't."

"Probably."

"I understand why she killed all of those people. At least some of them. I think she might have thought she was rescuing me. But, why did she whisper in that guy's ear about your brother's friend? That was what led to me leaving her. She had killed to get me back. Why initiate something that would take me away?"

"She couldn't have guessed that I would suggest merging our two families."

"You suggested that?" Kuroi asked surprised.

"Yeah. Did you think it was Sato?"

"He had traded me away so easily before. I just assumed he had again."

"No. Not this time."

"So, she's dead because she underestimated you," Kuroi said with the hint of a prideful smile.

"She isn't the first," I told him thinking of Uncle Vinny and all of the ones before him.

Regarding my father's reaction to what I had done, I was still waiting for it. But there was no longer a question about which of us was in charge. And with Uncle Vinny dead, he was out of surprise allies.

I was pretty sure he wouldn't just roll over and take what I had done because it wasn't his way. But his options were limited. As long as I stayed on top of things, I would remain a step ahead.

I was going to need Kuroi's help with that. Yeah, Matteo had made his loyalties clear. But my father's grip on him had always been strong. As long as Pa was alive, Matteo was a threat. My brother needed our father's approval too much for him not to be. Kuroi and I would need to keep an eye on Matteo too.

The last person I needed to figure out in all of this was what to do with Sato. He was going to die at my hands. There was no other way that this was gonna end. But his layers of security meant that it would take time. I was willing to wait.

What I hadn't had to wait long for was for Kuroi to again crave my cock.

"Haven't I been good lately?" he asked me one night after dinner.

We had just finished a steak that he had implied he cooked, but what I was pretty sure came from Alberto's, my favorite steak place. It didn't matter, though. He knew I couldn't resist him.

Now that we knew he wasn't a spider demon, it wasn't hard to figure out what power he had. His mother was a succubus. Kuroi didn't need to drain the life force from humans to survive, but he had inherited his mother's seductive power.

It explained everything that had happened to him since his power emerged at puberty. Not only did his sister want to possess him, every man wanted to fuck him. Who knows, maybe that was why Sato kept giving him away, to resist the temptation.

Luckily, as a wolf, I could only feel a fraction of its effects. Don't get me wrong, looking at him still made my cock hard. But, it was nowhere near what humans felt.

A part of me felt bad that my baby had to go through everything he had. And I wish I could feel more. But the other part was too busy thinking of all of the fucked up dirty things that I would do to him.

"You have been good. I've been impressed," I told him hoping I knew where this was going.

I had missed feeling his tight ass around my cock. I had even begun imagining the marks various household items would leave on his perfect skin.

"Didn't you once tell me, if I was good, you would reward me?"

"Do you think you were good enough to earn a reward?" I asked unable to suppress the smile creeping across my face.

"I don't know. Have I been?" he asked tilting his head and staring at me in a way that made my cock brick hard.

"I think you have," I confirmed before getting up and crossing the room to a closet.

As he watched me, I reached in and retrieved something I had bought for just this occasion. When I pulled it out and turned, his eyes lit up.

"Do you remember the safe word?" I asked the man I would love until the day I died.

He did. So, I began.

1) Sign up for the author's website BookishBoyfriend.com to get the sexy scene that follows for free! Getting the exclusive epilogue sex scene is easy. Simply go to BookishBoyfriend.com, and sign up for it like you would an author newsletter. Once in, click on Kuroi, and then click the **'Book Talk'** prompt, **'Spider Demon's Kiss - Epilogue - Sex Scene'**. It will pop right up!

2) Once you've read the short story, there are a few things you can do at BookishBoyfriend.com. I recommend having a steamy chat with Dante and Kuroi. You can try it out for free. And they only get NSFW when you want them to. ;-) Click here to get the exclusive short story now.

3) If you would like to get the alternative sex scenes for chapter 8 & 11, become a Patron member at BookishBoyfriend.com. Not only will becoming a Patron help support the author, but it will give you access to more of the author's exclusive short stories.

4) And if you would like to read the Wolf shifter variation of this book, as well as the author's previous books and variations, become a Premium member. Reading the books on BookishBoyfriend.com is cheaper than purchasing the books individually and you can unsubscribe anytime. Click here to go there now.

*****

Sneak Peek:
Enjoy this Sneak Peek of 'His Wolf Protector':

His Wolf Protector
(M/M Wolf Shifter)
By
Alex McAnders

Copyright 2023 McAnders Publishing
All Rights Reserved

Dillon Harris:

The last thing I expected to learn when I confronted my deadbeat dad was that he had a dark secret -- He was a vampire. How could that be? Dead men can't have children. So, how can I exist? And what am I?

Luckily, I have Remy to help me unravel this mystery. He's my best friend's wolf shifter brother, and although I was his little brother's human gay friend, he has always made me feel like I mattered. At least, I thought I had him until his mafia family's wolf pack rival forced Remy into an engagement with the alpha's daughter.

Wait, did I say I was human? Scratch that. I'm whatever it is that can see through the glamour magical creatures use to hide from the human world. That makes me the most dangerous magical creature in New York City... especially to whoever ordered my father to compel my mother to believe she was pregnant.

And now I have no one to protect me. Although, from the way Remy undresses me with his eyes, maybe I do.

Am I a lone pawn in a larger game to bring down humanity? Or is Remy, not just the man I've loved since the moment we met, but the knight who will save me from it all?

*****

His Wolf Protector

"Dillon, I've been in love with you for so long. From the moment I met you, I could never get enough. Every time you came by to hang out with Hil, I wondered if you saw me. So, when I had you so close, when I had everything I ever wanted in my arms, I was the happiest I could ever be.

"When you left me, I tried living without you. I knew by doing it I would keep everyone here safe. But the request was too much. I can't stay away from you, Dillon. I need you. I'm here to tell you that if you'll have me, I will never leave you again."

I gathered my emotions, trying to reign in the overwhelming wave threatening to crash.

"Remy," I began softly, "I left you for a reason. You have to be with Eris. Everyone's life depends on it. And even if it didn't, I can't be the other woman… or guy… or whatever. If I could, I'd do it for you. But I can't. I'm sorry!"

"But that's why I'm here," Remy explained. "I know I can't just walk away from Eris. But I also can't live without you," Remy declared baring his heart. "So I'm here to again ask for your help. I don't have all the answers like my father did. And I'm not him, I can't do this alone. I need the help of the people I love. And I love you."
Read more now

Sneak Peek:
Enjoy this Sneak Peek of 'His Caged Wolf':

His Caged Wolf
(M/M Wolf Shifter)
By
Alex McAnders

I was a lone wolf without a pack— could my fated mate be a human?

I don't know what it is about Cage Rucker that makes my wolf howl. Yeah, he has a body that's been chiseled from marble, and a smile that melts my heart, but it's more than that. There's something about the way he smells. My wolf knows.

Does that mean that this boy is going to fall all over himself to find out? No way. Cage has a girlfriend. I don't fall for straight boy… anymore. I wouldn't even have talked to him again if he hadn't offered me an exchange I couldn't refuse.

And now that I'm seeing him every day and he's making my wolf go wild, what am I supposed to do? I've worked tirelessly to suppress my wolf since it got loose and killed someone. Can I trust it now? Can I trust myself around Cage considering the way he makes me feel? Will I have a choice when I learn his secret?

I used to think I'm the only wolf shifter in existence. Am I be wrong? Could Cage be my fated mate?

'Caged Wolf' is a scorching hot MM wolf shifter romance with laughs, crackling tension, and enough spicy sizzle to leave you satisfied at its HEA ending.

His Caged Wolf

I looked up. He was right. The night was perfectly clear. There was nothing between us and the light of the full moon. How had I not remembered that tonight was the full moon?

It's not like it mattered. I wasn't a hollowing monster enslaved by it. I hadn't shifted in years. I had long ago gotten control over myself, over my body. I was Quin Toro, human, not some mindless wolf…

"You cold?"

"What?"

"You're shivering."

I was shaking. "I guess I'm nervous," I admitted.

"What are you nervous about?"

My face got hot. "I don't know."

Cage stared at me. "You're a good-looking guy. Do you know that?"

"So are you," I told him shaking even more.

"Thanks. Are you happy you came out tonight?"

"Yeah, definitely," I said fighting not to show him how much.

"We're here," he said as we approached the door of my building.

"We're here," I repeated my heart pounding. "Do you want to come in?"

"Come in?" Cage asked caught off guard.

"Yes," I replied struggling not to pounce him right there.

 "Ahhhh," he murmured before the door popped open and a girl came out.

"Cage!" She said before wrapping her arms around him and standing on her tiptoes to kiss his lips.

My mouth dropped open in shock. What was going on? What had just happened?

The petite, blonde with angular features turned towards me. "Who's this?"

"Ah, this is Quin. Quin this is Tasha."

Tasha looked at me suspiciously while Cage became uncomfortable.

"Tasha is my girlfriend."

"How do you know Cage?" Tasha asked me.

I was too shocked by everything to speak.

"Quin had asked me for a selfie."

Tasha turned to Cage surprised. "Oh. Did you give him one?"

"Not yet," Cage said with a smile.

"I can take it," Tasha volunteered. "Give me your phone," she said approaching me with her hand out.

Still speechless, I handed her my phone and stood next to Cage.

"Say cheese," she said.

"Cheese," Cage replied while I stared back stunned.

"Here you go," she said handing me back my phone. "Check it."

I looked down and saw my full humiliation on display. "Yes."

"Okay. Let's go. I'm hungry," Tasha said entwining her body with Cage's and pulling him away.

"It was nice meeting you, Quin," he said looking at me as he left.

"Yes. It was nice meeting… you," I mumbled sure that he could no longer hear me.

I watched as the perfectly suited couple walked off. Of course, he had a girlfriend. And, of course, she looked like that. My heart hurt watching them go.

I can't believe I thought he was interested in me. No one's ever interested in me. How could I have been so foolish? How could I think a guy like him could be interested in a guy like me?

Once the two had disappeared into the darkness, I entered the building. Ascending the stairs in a daze, I felt like I was going to explode. Why didn't anyone ever like me back? Why didn't Cage like me?

I couldn't take this anymore. My skin vibrated with a ferocity I hadn't felt in years. When I finally realized what was going on, it was too late.

"Oh no. No, no, no, no, no," I said in a panic.

As I bound up the stairs, the world around me drifted further away. I needed to lock myself up. I couldn't believe this. It had been years. Why now? Why here?

Approaching my dorm room door, I smelled the last thing I wanted to smell or expected. Lou was home. Why was he home? Didn't he say he had a date?

I didn't want him to see me like this. I didn't want to terrify him with the truth of who I was. I didn't want to accidently kill him.

Was this how my mother died? Had I lost control and ripped out her throat? I was too young to remember. But a three-year-old child and a three-year-old wolf are different. If I let it, would the beast inside of me hurt another person I cared about?

I couldn't let it. But how could I stop it?
Read more now

*****

*****